Enjoy Me

ENJOY ME

Logan Ryan Smith

Transmission Press
Chicago, Illinois

First Edition

Transmission Press, Chicago 60625

Printed in the United States of America

"Bret Easton Ellis" first appeared in *Great Lakes Review*, Issue 2, Spring 2013 (nominated for a Pushcart Prize); "Blue Monster" first appeared in *Meat For Tea: The Valley Review*, Volume 7, Issue Four.

24 23 22 21 20 19 18 17 16 15   1 2 3 4 5

ISBN-13: 978-1-505-55333-8
ISBN-10: 1505553334

for Abby, Storma, and Summer
with apologies
for the disparagement

Oh, it's a strange day
In such a lonely way
Some people look down on me
I know they like what they see
—New Order, *Truth*

Please don't turn me off
I don't know what I'm doing outside
Me and the telephone that never rings
If you were me, what would you do?
Me, I disconnect from you
—Tubeway Army, *Me! I Disconnect From You*

I just want to give you the creeps
Run and hide when I'm on the streets
Your fears and your tears
I'll taunt you in your sleep
I just want to give you the creeps
—Social Distortion, *The Creeps*

I've got the spirit, but lose the feeling
—Joy Division, *Disorder*

STORIES

ENJOY ME

The noise of crickets chirping is enormous and shattering, threatening to crack the glass of Jim Beam I hold in my hand that's on the bar of Bourbon Bandits, my usual place, which is dark and was cool 30 minutes ago but has been getting warmer, muggier, and more claustrophobic as the crickets' crescendo grows louder and louder as the conductor, standing before them on long, skinny black legs sprouting shards of black hair, urges this movement to its climax, louder and louder, each cricket's sound bouncing off the other, louder and louder, until it's overwhelming and incomprehensible as the sound becomes an inescapable whirring, painful, and monotonous note.

Then it's just the murmur of the people around me smelling of patchouli and shower-less days, yet full of a confidence given them by their young peers that's informed them, erroneously, that the human body isn't a disgusting, vile thing.

I stare at my glass of Jim Beam and try to hear the Joy Division song I put on the Internet jukebox more than 30 minutes ago but just now comes on. The chatter, chanting, and yelling of San Francisco's youngest and brightest—the future artists, authors, musicians, and pederasts—overtakes the song's melancholy lull, and I can only hear a stray bass line from Peter Hook and a barely intelligible mutter from Ian Curtis. I can't even tell what song it is because I can't remember which song I played and I'm on my fourth glass of Jim Beam.

The bartender comes up to me. He's blurry, on a pair of long, thin black cricket legs that make music as they slide against each other.

"Hey, Luke," Stan says.

"Yeah?" I don't look at him, keeping my focus on my glass while trying to figure out what Joy Division song it was I played.

"Listen, I'm splitting. My shift is almost over. Mind if we close out?" he says, holding up the credit card I handed him when I took a seat here about an hour and a half ago.

"Who's coming in?" I ask, swirling the ice in my drink, not making eye contact, surprised I can hear Stan over the babble.

Someone screams "Shot!" and for a second I'm thinking—hoping—someone's pulled a gun and started shooting the place up, but it's just a couple of kids near the open door slamming their tequilas down and calling for another.

I try to hide my immense disappointment from Stan, who I like well enough as he's a good bartender, keeps my drinks flowing, and comps me plenty because I've been coming here long enough for him to think he knows me.

"Hey!" Stan says, snapping little furry fingers in front of my face. "Can I close out your tab, or not? I gotta go, man."

"Who's coming in?" I repeat, raising my voice.

"Um," he says, backing up from the bar, thinking hard to remember who's replacing him. "Oh, I think it's Cameron."

"No," I say.

"No, what, Luke?"

"No, you can't close out my tab. I'm not going anywhere. I'm staying right here."

"Listen, man, I need you to close out so I can get out of here."

"Fine," I say. "Close me out but keep my card back there. I'm not going anywhere."

In stop-motion, large crickets hop in and out of the stools at the bar around me. Most have tattoos and smell like B.O. and some say things to me like "excuse me" and "hey, don't I know you" and "I dug the reading you gave last week" and I mostly ignore these people infiltrating my space, shrug, and maybe smile a little to keep them away from me.

Stan shuffles away with my card, runs my bill, I sign the slip and tip well. Stan looks at the tip I've written down and doesn't say anything, has no noticeable reaction to the fact I've tipped him 40% of my total tab. But that doesn't bother me too much as I've gotten used to the fact that no one really appreciates generosity and gratitude has long been dead.

Yeah, the only mistake was that you ran away... is the first bit of lyrics I hear from the Internet jukebox. "The Only Mistake". I'm not sure why I played that song. It's not one of my favorites.

I step out of Bourbon Bandits onto the sidewalk of Geary Street and take my place among the zombies and psychopaths. How do I tell the difference? The psychopaths wear suits. The zombies have skin peeling off their faces and reek of rotting teeth and were likely the extras in a movie we were all in but forgot about.

I light a Winston as Cameron comes out of the door next to Bourbon Bandits. She shuts the security door. She's wearing skinny jeans. Black. To match her long dark hair and bangs. Her pale shoulders and thin arms exposed because of her tight, flimsy white tank top. Her left arm's tattooed with a large, blue monster I've always tried to ignore.

"Hi, Luke!" she says as she bounces past me. "Back again, huh?"

I'm 31-years-old, living in San Francisco, currently unemployed, collecting money from the government and the few bucks I get from magazines that publish my short stories and poetry. I've achieved nothing so far. I've written stories and poems, but no books and nothing that's made me real money or scored me a teaching gig. I have no children and haven't had a relationship last more than 6 months since I was 23. I have three or four imaginary friends that I only like because their poetry is pretty good.

A zombie bumps shoulders with me and his jaw breaks off and falls against the cement. The few teeth that were left in it fall out, clink against the sidewalk like so many black pennies. Finally, the jingling comes to a stop as some roll into the gutter. I don't pick up the jaw or his teeth since he barley notices and keeps shuffling on up toward Van Ness.

"Fucking asshole," I mutter.

"Excuse me?" Cameron asks, her eyes big with the excitement of confrontation.

I look in through the open door of the bar, then back to Cameron, "Oh, no. Sorry. I wasn't talking to you, of course. Um, could you get that *asshole* out of my chair?" I ask, motioning inside toward the douchebag sitting patiently in my seat where my drink waits for me as he waits for Cameron to show up and pour *him* a drink.

Cameron looks at me, confused, but then agrees to get the guy out of my seat, smiles and walks her tight ass into the bar.

Because I've wanted to fuck Cameron since she started working at Bourbon Bandits about six months ago I pull out a small plastic bag from my pocket, then my keys, and sneak a bump—though, really, there's no reason for my subtlety as right when I replace the bag I see a zombie across the street in front of the Peruvian deli, squatting against their windows with a needle dangling out of his arm, shaking violently. The diners inside the deli pretend not to notice as his arm falls off and shatters on the ground. Then he's lying in front of the building with just one arm, sleeping, apparently. Passersby step over him, kicking up the dust of his shattered arm.

It's not late yet. Only nine o'clock or so. Cameron is behind the bar, and like a good bartender, she's cleared my seat for me.

As I walk in and push past a mass of cricket mandibles vibrating uselessly, push past all these insects hopping haphazardly from table to booth to chair and to the back area to shoot some pool, I feel sick. I go down to one knee, put a hand on one of the cricket's disgusting, shimmering legs, and get kicked away.

Before the wave of nausea can envelope me, I swallow it back and taste bile in the back of my mouth, then a spindle of stomach acid unravels from my stomach and scorches the soft palate of my mouth. Someone helps me up. A soft voice that says, "Are you okay?" I don't respond, just take my spot at the bar. I wonder if I should do more coke.

Then the bar clears out. Almost completely empty. It's Friday night and I have nothing else to do and like it this way and Cameron is here so I stay. I don't want to leave.

I down my glass of Jim Beam and am pleased I can hear Depeche Mode's "Behind the Wheel" playing crystal clear from the Internet jukebox. I find a little too much pleasure in my anxiety to find out what I might have played next.

"Where'd everybody go?" I ask Cameron as she cleans glasses.

Giant lizards are eating rancid rats on the TV screens at each end of the bar, sucking out their eyeballs first before shoving their scaly muzzles into the rats' open and bloated bellies and flicking their long tongues down the rats' ears, testing their brains. A flashing neon light in the middle of the bar reads "Enjoy Me" below a beer's logo I've never seen before.

"I think LCD Sound System is playing over at the Great American," she says, barely looking up from washing those grimy pint glasses.

"Oh, yeah?" I ask, not really caring. "Who's opening?"

She smiles, "Shitty City Titty Twister."

"Ah, well, there's the real draw, I say," smiling, making sure we make eye contact and that she realizes I'm the only one in the bar.

She gives me a quizzical look and I hear the splat of zombies outside vomiting their lungs out against the pavement and losing their bowels in the middle of the street.

"What?" I ask. "I'm not funny?"

"Uh, not sure what's funny there, Luke," she says, putting glasses away and moving down the bar.

"So, you can make a joke that's not even a joke, but I can't respond with something equally unfunny and get a smile out of you?"

"Just finish your drink, Luke."

"Quit saying my name," I say, under my breath.

"Huh?"

"Nothing."

The TV now shows lions humping, then devouring antelopes. Large red ribbons of flesh open up on the screen, but no blood sprays the way you'd expect to see in a movie. But I'm not sure if I'm watching a movie or a reality program.

I light up a Winston at the bar, finish my drink like I'm told to do, and ask for another.

"Come on, Luke, you know there's no smoking in here," Cameron says as she grabs my empty glass and fills it.

"Come on, *Cameron*, no one's here," I complain.

She looks at me, perplexed, and antennae grow out of her forehead and her mandibles flitter back and forth something unintelligible as her legs push together, making an intolerable sound, while the TV shows a fuzzy video of a naked girl in a bed, her ankles tied to the bedposts, her arms tied behind her back, her face covered by a George W. Bush mask. Two men, stark naked, stand opposite each other, bedside. One wears a Hitler mask with a grotesquely large, pink grin, and the other wears an oversized Simon Cowell mask, though I'm not entirely sure if it's a mask or actually Simon Cowell. It probably is Simon Cowell, I tell myself, and it's Simon Cowell that's holding a large, serrated knife. He holds it before him, turns and looks up at the corner of the room where the camera is filming it all, shows us the knife, then turns the knife on himself and slices off his left hand, slowly, cutting through tendon and bone. He falls to one knee, the hand with the knife in it on the bed, the other hand rolling under the bed, and the girl on the bed in the George W. Bush mask writhes against her restraints, but we can't hear anything from the TV, only the Soft Cell song, "Sex Dwarf," that I put on earlier, now finally playing.

I'm wondering why Cameron doesn't watch this, doesn't notice the TV and how intently I'm watching it. Then Simon Cowell, seemingly about to lose consciousness, stands back up, takes the knife and thrusts it into George W. Bush's neck, her tits swaying violently for less than 15 seconds before coming to a complete halt. Then Hitler and Simon Cowell have sex in the blood-soaked bed, George W. Bush pushed off to the side, dangling off the bed, arms tied behind the back, legs still tied to the bed posts.

I turn my head away and Cameron is staring at *me* intently.

"Put. It. Out. Luke. Now," she says.

I shake myself out of my stupor and remember how beautiful she is and how little I know about her. She's fuming right now and I can't stop looking at her. But I find a nearby glass with a little bit of beer left in it, take one last quick drag and drop the mostly unsmoked cigarette into the glass.

Blowing the smoke out the side of my face where I believe a hole has been developing over the last two years, I say,

"Happy?" I smile and when I do I notice one of my front teeth is missing, though I can't recall when that happened.

Cameron just smiles back at me and says she is. When I look back at the TV there's a commercial of a bunch of jack rabbits making fun of a rattlesnake that has a baby rattle at the end of his tail instead of the rattle it should have been born with. They're all laughing at the snake as he tries to be menacing.

I feel a passing sense of empathy.

The Nine Inch Nails song, "Closer," comes on the Internet jukebox and I sing along, watching Cameron down at the other end of the bar, cleaning glasses, and I'm trying to be jovial and playful by putting a lounge-singer twist on the chorus of "I want to fuck you like an animal!" but Cameron either can't hear me or is ignoring me because her eyes don't even look my way.

Suddenly I remember the pocket knife a friend left at my place one night. It's in my pocket, where it's supposed to be, though it isn't mine. I've been meaning to give it back, keeping it on me in case I ran into him. But I think he moved to Berlin. Or Bakersfield. I'm not sure.

"Enjoy Me" flickers in the middle of the bar and I catch a glimpse of myself in the mirror. My snout has grown wider and my forehooves look infected and swollen. The small patch of hair atop my pink head, I swear, right now, in this bar light, looks like it's gone fucking grey. But I'm positive it was still dark brown this morning.

I look around the bar, remind myself that no one is here

but me and Cameron. I look at the TV. It's just a basketball game. The door's open and the dark night outside seeps in. Blackness—more of it comes into the room and I hear the moans of the zombies strolling Geary Street outside, increasing. It's almost like coyotes, but only if the coyotes had already had their throats slit before having a hand forcefully shoved through the skin of their bellies where fingers play with their intestines and break through the wall of their stomachs, finding that the impaled has had so little to eat.

"Enjoy Me."

I grab my drink, pull out another cigarette—not to light, just to taunt—and walk down to the end of the bar Cameron is at.

"Hi, Luke," she says, working the glasses behind the bar, though I'm trying to figure out why she still has so many glasses to clean since the bar has been nearly empty except for myself for the last 45 minutes or more.

"Quit. Saying. My. Name," I say, then smile.

"What?" she doesn't look up at me.

Outside: sirens. Gunshots. Multiple wounded. Guts on the street. Just a little further east on down the street. Maybe down on Leavenworth. Someone is clutching their chest and fighting for breath as flashing red, white, and blue lights parade over them. One cop laughs and says, bending over the fella clutching his chest, "This one's bit the dust!" And the guy screams, "No! No I haven't! Help me! *Help* me!" and the blood gets darker on his chest as he screams and is thrown into the meat wagon and the meat wagon speeds off, all sound fading, and the lights in the back of the meat wagon turn off.

"Nothing," I say. "You know, Cameron…." I take a drink of the Jim Beam, fumble the Winston between my fingers, and wonder what it'd be like to light it, smoke it halfway down, despite her protests, and shove it into her eye.

"What, Luke?"

I settle myself, take a breath, try to control the urge to lash out, knowing I've already asked her a couple times not to say my name.

"I've always liked you, Cameron," I say, purposefully mentioning *her* name.

"That's nice, Luke." She's still not looking at me.

"I don't think you heard me."

"Huh?"

"I said I don't think you heard me, *Cameron*."

"No, Luke, I heard you."

"What's your problem then?"

"I don't have a problem. I heard you. Just drop it, okay? And don't light that cigarette. I'm warning you."

I pull out my lighter just to tease her but she doesn't find it funny.

Morrissey's "Suedehead" comes on and I'm lulled by false sentimentality, forgetting what I was doing or why I'm here.

I hear crickets chirping, making out with zombies outside

Bourbon Bandits' open door. I hear parts of bodies falling apart. Lungs are destroyed by the chitter-chatter of unmanageable and toothless jaws. I don't know how long it's been, but there's too many of them outside and I know the concert hasn't ended by now.

On the TV is a headless singer. I don't get it.

Passersby push baby carriages. I don't get it. It must be nearly midnight by now. Why are people pushing their babies around Geary Street at midnight when all the zombies and crickets and cops and monsters are out? Why are they taking their babies out at this time and in this place? I can only assume occultism. I can only fathom that this city is run by yuppies that worship Satan and sacrifice children.

I realize I'm standing in the threshold of Bourbon Bandits, my cigarette lit, half smoked, though I don't remember smoking it.

I look back at Cameron. She's watching the TV. It's a computer-generated cartoon of a dragon and a girl is riding it over the oceans. The dragon takes a sharp right turn and the girl falls off, hundreds of feet down, cracking her skull open on the ocean. The ocean, it looks so soft, but it breaks this animated girl's head wide open. Her brain falls out like the yolk of an egg and drops to the sea's floor. From it grow cities in which everyone is sentenced to die.

I throw my cigarette out the door, notice the zombie with the missing arm is still asleep against the Israeli Café. Cars zip by. Rain is on the way. I walk back to where Cameron is working behind the bar, doing God-knows-what now.

"Why don't you like me?" I snort, one misshapen pink hoof on the bar, the other clutching tightly to my drink.

"Please. You've had enough. No more for you, buck-o," she says, motioning for me to exit.

"I need to know! Why don't you like me! What's *wrong* with me?"

"Luke, listen, get out now before I call the owner. He lives right upstairs. He'll 86 your ass and then what will you do? Where will you go?"

"Cameron, *please*!" I'm begging. I notice in the mirror across from me that tears have begun to form in my large, round eyes.

"Out. Right fucking now, Luke," she says coldly.

"Please, Cameron. No! Don't kick me out! Please!"

Cameron shoots a look of both astonishment and bewilderment. Harried, she searches for her cell phone in her pockets, behind the bar, between bottles of Fernet Branca.

I finger the pocket knife in my pocket.

She can't seem to find her phone. She looks puzzled, reserved, almost ready to give up.

"Do… I have to go?" I ask.

"Yes, Luke," she says, tired. "Please. Just go. You can come back tomorrow. But please just go. You've had too much."

"But you don't know what's out there! They're trying to

get me! All of them! Fucking monsters! The *monsters*, Cameron!"

Across from me, in the mirror, I'm tearing at my eyes and blood streams from them. My mouth is wet and red and pleading.

She walks toward the landline phone.

I won't move. I won't budge. I'm not going out there. I take a seat, light another cigarette, and hold my drink in a shaky hand.

"Out! Now!" she says walking back toward me. "The owner's on his way. He'll be here any second, and while maybe I won't call the cops on you, he will."

I drop my cigarette, and somehow I completely lose it.

Cameron's long, slender cricket body vibrates. She grows wings that beat violently, and I can taste it in the air: her fear. The sharp hairs on her legs start making music that sound like Vivaldi, but more modern, like Vivaldi was suddenly writing music for bad movies.

"I won't! I won't go! I won't do it! You can't make me! Please, Cameron! Please let me stay!"

Her eyes look away, down toward the entrance, and I realize there are others here. Just a few. I have no idea how long they've been here. Perhaps a long while.

There's a cricket, quivering and senseless, bent over a low table right near the bar's narrow entrance, and there's a zombie, its face skinless, abrasions and sores all over its arms and chest, grey and hideous, fucking the cricket from behind, becoming more violent with each thrust as the dark keeps moving in.

A Robert Palmer song, which I did not put on the Internet jukebox, is playing: "I Didn't Mean to Turn You On".

The building starts shaking and the bad art falls off the black walls. The couple fucking at the front of the bar don't notice and keep on until the zombie's dick breaks off inside the cricket and they're both screaming as he pulls away from her, stumbling and bleeding.

"Listen," Cameron whispers, now touching my wrist over the bar, something in her switching on as she watches the guy walk out of the bar, pulling his pants up ridiculously, clutching his crotch and screaming. And the girl bent over the table laughs, stands up, puts the bloody pocket knife between her tits, pulls her skirt down, and exits.

"You can stay. Just calm the fuck down, okay?" Cameron says.

"I can? I can stay?" I say, my tears coming to an immediate halt, my lips stretching across my wide teeth as I grin painfully hard.

"Yes. Yes. Just… don't leave me here alone with these monsters," she says quietly, reaching across the bar and absentmindedly grabbing my hand.

I shudder inside at the contact. I quake. Nearly collapse completely at her touch. My heart grows heavy and sinks down into my guts and swirls. It hurts so much. It feels so good. I hold back new tears and pat her hand, consolingly.

Wild yells and yelps escape down the street outside. Sirens wail. Pieces of bodies roll in and out of the bar as if we're inside a pinball machine.

I grab my glass of Jim Beam.

"Okay. Okay. Yeah, alright. I don't have to leave?"

"No. No, Luke. Please stay," she says in a small voice, visibly upset. "Just stay for a little while, okay? Here, I'll get you another drink."

Completely distracted, her eyes on the door, she pours me another drink. I light a cigarette and she says nothing.

The TV now shows sweeping green landscapes of either Ireland or Iceland or some place that starts with an 'I'. Every now and again, through the beauty of the place, I see the bones of broken hands reaching through the earth, some missing fingers, some with hooves, instead, kicking through the dirt. Faces pushing against the soil, sobbing and broken-hearted. Bodies falling apart against the beauty of the sun just now rising. Disintegrating. Turning to dust. Bodies just fading away into nothingness.

I look up and see "Enjoy Me Enjoy Me Enjoy Me" flashing over and over again.

I take my seat at the bar and look at Cameron, take hold of my drink, and try not to cry from the gratitude.

CAMERON WASHES GLASSES

Depeche Mode's "Blasphemous Rumors" plays on the juke in Bourbon Bandits as the TV mutely replays the story from last night about a young church-going couple shot to death while sleeping on Stinson Beach. I sip my Lagunitas IPA, watch Cameron wash glasses, her thin arms moving up and down like pistons. In my head I can see the 20-something couple giggly on the beach. I can hear the Pacific lick the sands so near them, calling them into it though they'll never come. Then I hear them say, *no*, they'll wait, they'll wait for a more appropriate time to fuck—though they don't use that word—and they touch each other's faces like they love each other and look into each other's eyes with such longing not knowing that that longing is spawned from not fucking and if they had fucked already they'd likely not be on the beach right now under stars, pretending, with the sound of waves wrapped around them and arms wrapped around each other for warmth with legs rubbing like cricket legs for song while blood flows and body parts swell and hearts beat hard in order to say *no.* No, they'd be somewhere fucking, behind closed doors and not on a beach eventually falling asleep from the exhaustion of resisting temptation, of being faithful to the words of their parents, their churches, and themselves. And instead of the act of penetrating and being penetrated, instead they fall asleep under blue moonlight near a quaking ocean and western winds that carry clean salt and each get shot in the face only seconds apart.

And then I see Cameron behind the bar touching herself with her eyes closed, moaning.

It takes a moment, but I finally realize she's just washing more glasses, humming to the song. I look around the bar and it's empty except for Old Man Bill sitting in the back at a table under an oil painting of a greased-up, well-built boxer in the standard pose. Only this boxer has Bill's old head attached to that adroit physique.

Old Man Bill looks at me. I look at him. He laughs. I look back at my Lagunitas IPA and drink. I throw $5 on the bar, look back at Cameron, who doesn't look at me, and exit the bar into the bright 3 p.m. San Francisco sunlight and all the shit-stained glory of Geary Street and the Tenderloin.

A one-armed, cross-eyed man hobbles over to me, asks for change, his breath smelling of week-old tuna and rancid spinach. Before receiving an answer, though, he hobbles past me, yelling scripture, and trips, falls to the pavement and shatters into a million shards of glass.

I cough and light a cigarette and put on my Wayfarers. Somebody in a waist-apron scuttles out of a storefront with a dust pan and broom and sweeps up the mass of scattered shards, muttering obscenities, disgusted, before disappearing back into the store.

An airplane roars overhead and everybody stops what they're doing and looks up before moving on.

Fog is somewhere under the Golden Gate Bridge waiting to eat us all, but it's staying there, invisible, for the time being, waiting for the right hour to cover and consume us.

It's 2002 and the future isn't here yet. I take a look at the extremely thin, aged black man across the street with a needle in his arm, passed out in a non-descript doorway before pulling out my tiny bag of coke, taking a bit on my finger and rubbing it on my gums.

I don't move for five minutes until the world proves itself to be a brighter place full of promise.

I need a job so I walk over to the newspaper dispenser on the corner, pushing through 100 different versions of myself, each with a deformity, then put my 50 cents in and try to open it only to discover that yet again newspaper dispensers oppose me and don't want me to know what's going on in the world.

I jiggle it. I jammer it. I boggle it. I hit it. I hit it again. I kick it and it falls over into the street and the door pops open. I reach in, take my paper, close the door, hold up a hand for oncoming traffic and search the classifieds. Horns blare. Brakes squeal. Cars zip around me. Swear words are spat. And middle fingers are shown before being reinserted into their owner's ass or that of the passenger's.

The classifieds tell me I'm supposed to be using the Internet to find a job. I throw the paper into the street where 100 different deformed versions of myself run after it and fight for the paper's different sections. I wonder who ended up with the personals. I wonder which of us will be put out of my misery.

I get lonely so I wander back to Bourbon Bandits and peek inside and see Cameron getting fucked from behind at the bar by an eight-foot tall, obscenely muscular dude wearing only a football helmet. His body is webbed in thick, pulsing purple veins. His blue lips are pulled back into a grimace behind the facemask. He's got her long brown hair wrapped around his bulging forearm. Cameron's face is blissful, beautiful, barely shaken. Old Man Bill is in the back under his self-portrait, toothlessly laughing and clapping and banging his hand on the table. I close the door, take a drag of my Winston Light, notice the junky across the street is no longer there and the fog is slowly, painfully slowly, rolling over the low buildings across the street, just waiting.

I peek my head back inside the bar and Cameron's watching the TV showing again the story of the couple that had their brains blown into sand and she has the volume up and there's no one in the bar wearing a football helmet and Old Man Bill's nowhere to be seen.

Pictures of the couple are shown and they don't look older than 17 and I assume the news is lying about their age. Then I see moonlight falling on sand and hear waves crashing against it and driftwood hollowly banging against other driftwood. And I see feet moving forward in the whitewash, hiding footsteps in the sound of waves kissing the beach, and there's a couple up ahead and a gun in my hand and the couple is cuddled closely against each other, the Pacific wind gently pushing into the girl's hair, lifting it with invisible fingers, and, God, I feel so lonely and the moon is big and bright and there's no stars, there's never any stars, and the ocean is stupidly endless and dark, and the driftwood is getting louder, sounding like old bones fighting to make it out of bed to meet another day, and the couple—one of them snoring—is getting closer, lying there on the beach in their two sleeping bags zipped together as one, and they're so pretty and young and the world is crashing around them and they're so innocent, his hands on her face and her arms wrapped harmlessly around his middle. I see them at my feet, the waves telling me to just do it, that no one deserves this, that no one deserves anything and it's a lonely fucked up world and before I know it their heads explode beneath my feet before either has a chance to open an eye and for a second I feel grateful they went so peacefully.

Suddenly the sun sets and the fog drops and I'm covered

in ground clouds and dying light. One-hundred lame versions of myself bump into me on their way to more important places, such as hospitals, burial grounds, and open, welcoming legs. One of them turns to me, a mouth full of black spots, and says, "You're a real piece of work, you are," before tossing a quarter at me and moving on.

I drop the cigarette from my mouth that went out a long time ago, pick the quarter up off the sidewalk, and take off my Wayfarers.

Then I'm all alone on Geary. Nothing but me and the fog and the end of the day. I make a mental note to pay my Internet bill.

I pull out a cigarette and walk into Bourbon Bandits and Cameron tells me to take it outside. I finish the cigarette outside. It's 6 p.m. I go back inside. The bar is still empty and Cameron pours me a pint of whiskey and soda water. Old Man Bill sits below his portrait, telling jokes to himself about Polacks and laughing.

"Does he ever stop laughing?" I ask Cameron.

"Huh?" she says, as if she didn't even realize I was there. The TV has a picture of Old Man Bill on it and he's laughing. Then it's just the usual porn.

"Laughing. Does Old Man Bill ever stop laughing?" I ask.

"Um, I don't know, Luke," she says and starts washing more glasses, though I have no idea where all these dirty glasses are coming from when it's just me and Old Man Bill, and it looks to me like Cameron is touching herself so I avoid the TV and just watch Cameron wash glasses.

GREAT AMERICAN

The very early, dark morning pulls down around us as we stand outside of Aberdeen Tower on Geary Street enshrouded in a cloud of cigarette smoke, giving as many dirty looks to tight-pants-wearing walkers as those we're receiving.

A woman in a fur coat covered in blood pauses before us, talking on an ancient, bulky mobile phone as her dachshund takes a tiny shit. Then she moves on, leaving the steaming brown package behind.

"Let's go over to the Great American," Gem says.

"It's 2:30 a.m., Gem. It's closed," Sanchez, in his grey three-piece suit, says coolly through a fog of gin breath, a tall and skinny black-haired model in a tight glimmering white dress and heels clings to him, her eyelids heavy.

"I work there, dipshit. I have the keys," she says, dangling them in front of his face. She's had maybe eight Jameson and soda waters but she's not showing it.

Kevin's across the street smoking and looking down at us from his second-story apartment window. I motion for him to come down and join us. He flicks his cigarette out the window, spits and walks out of view.

I have visions of San Francisco burning down in mountain-high flames, which fills me with a momentary euphoria, but I walk out into the middle of the street anyway and nearly get hit by some silver foreign sports car speeding past as I stamp out Kevin's discarded butt.

"Jesus, be careful," Gem says as I return.

A stream of hoofed drunkards in large nose rings clod past us, snorting and running at red lights with their oversized rhinoceros heads aimed low. One of them charges the traffic light and meets the aerodynamic fender of another expensive foreign car and goes rolling over the top of the speeding vehicle and crashes to the asphalt in a torn up mess, blood squirting from a major artery in its inner thigh and dribbling from its muzzle and neck while it lies motionless, veiled in miasma.

Nobody does anything. Then one bystander up the street calls animal services. Later, in the morning light, they'll scrape it from the street and incinerate it in a grey cube of a building somewhere in Emeryville.

"What do you think, Luke?" Gem's drug dealer, Eric, asks. He's been tagging along all evening, playing Limp Bizkit on the juke and thinking it funny and making Cameron, who joined us earlier for a short time, grow nervous and leave.

"What do I *think*?" I ask.

"Yeah, want to go over to the Great American? Gem has keys." He fidgets, pulls the hood of his No Fear hoodie over his head and stuffs his hands in the pockets. Sniffles.

"I have ears, asshole," I say, and Eric guffaws.

"Well?" he asks.

"Jesus fucking Christ," I say, and take a drag from my Winston and look to see if Kevin's back at the window but he's not and the light's off.

I see ghosts in the shadows twist and turn and waver and I feel a coldness reach down into my throat, triggering my gag reflex, causing me to cough, nearly vomit.

Gem's on her phone calling friends and my small crowd of glitterati moves up around the corner to the Great American Music Hall where I once took Serena to see Neutral Milk Hotel. We sat up in the mezzanine, in the seats farthest in the back, and while the sound poured over us she let me put my fingers inside her, and, after, as we were about to leave, she said "thank you" and "I love you" before using her connections in the music world to get back stage where I was not allowed to go. Then I left and never heard from her again.

"So you're a poet, right?" Eric asks, dropping back to where I'm tailing.

I smirk, nearly throw up, cough a few times, take a drag from my Winston, and say, "Don't you know it."

And Eric laughs.

"Listen, man. You're alright, man," he says, still chuckling.

I envision putting an ax into the back of his neck, but only halfway, out of pity.

Out in front of the Great American, Sanchez and his date make out and Gem fumbles with her keys as five tattooed, pierced-up, snarling 20-somethings hop, skip and jump toward us yelling, "Ge-em! Ge-em! Come out and play-ee-ay!"

And when they're close enough, Gem giggles and hugs each of them, folds into all of their arms like soft origami, the blue moonlight spilling over us, and they all seem to care about each other profusely and I just try not to dry heave or pass out.

As we push behind Gem through the first set of doors, and then the second, we become immersed in pitch blackness. No one says anything as Gem curses, seems to bump into something, curses again. Then there's a series of clicks and slowly the music hall begins to glow before us, its ornate gold ceiling and mezzanine, the red walls and pillars, and the wood floor stretching before us toward the stage.

"Hold on," Gem says, putting a finger of warning up, then disappearing into a room behind the bar, off to the side, as all of us stand still, unwilling to disobey her order while the place around us warms up in light.

Suddenly Janet Jackson blares from the speakers around the hall and Gem comes running out laughing from her hiding place and starts dancing on the wood floor where Sanchez and his date and the party of fanciful tattooed kids join her.

I walk behind the bar, search around and find the plastic cups, and watch everyone dance on the floor to "What Have You Done for Me Lately". I pull myself a foamy cup of Anchor Steam Pale Ale and sip it, light up another Winston, look at my phone and see that I've missed no calls, no text messages.

One tall kid with long brown hair and the left side of his head shaved runs over and says, "You the 'tender?"

"I'm behind the bar," I say and keep my place.

"Mind pouring me a PBR?" he asks over the enormous beats.

I look around, make a motion that says, *take in your surroundings, jackass*, and explain, "You know, this is all free. You can have whatever you want."

He gives me a confused look. I sip my pale ale, pour myself a shot of Maker's Mark, then pour the sad sap a PBR and lean back behind the bar, watch this girl with long red hair in a short black dress and blue eyeliner dance. I hadn't seen her among the troupe of the tattooed and realize she must have come in after us. She moves with lithe motion, sexual and controlled. She's laughing hard, her neck bent back, beautiful as a misshapen tree winding out of the swamp. Then I see Eric passing out bumps and I perk up, lean against the bar as all on the dance floor partake.

The song ends and the hall fills with the sound of chickens clucking and ruffling feathers before the harmony of a thousand birds being slaughtered decks the halls. Eric sees me behind the bar and sort of jogs over to me through a snowfall of red feathers, though no one seems to notice them.

"Hey, wordsmith. Want some?" he asks, motioning to a very tiny plastic bag of white powder.

"I ain't paying for it," I say.

He chuckles and offers the bag to me. I take out my keys, dip in and indulge.

He laughs again and says, "Hey, can you pour me a PBR?"

A Debbie Gibson song bursts overhead. Debbie Gibson—the first female singer I'd ever obsessed over. I was eight-years-old and in love in a way I haven't been since. I wonder what Debbie's up to these days.

Before getting the PBR, I look around, and to my surprise find a half-full bottle of Black Maple Hill 23-year-old Kentucky rye behind a package of paper towels. I mix up a couple manhattans in plastic martini glasses then take a straight shot from the bottle. Next, I look around again for the plastic cups, pull one from the bag and throw it at Eric, say, "Get it yourself, douchebag," and make my way out to the dance floor with the manhattans.

"Only in My Dreams" blasts overhead and things start to brighten.

Gem dances with me before realizing I'm standing as still as a fence post trying not to spill the drinks, then she guffaws and gently pushes me away, moves on. I'm looking at the redhead but she's now dancing with Sanchez and his date is off leaning against one of the red pillars, pouting.

I step in between Sanchez and the redhead. "Hi," I say, and hand her the drink. I look at Sanchez and motion with my eyes in the direction of his date, which he quickly understands and so leaves us alone.

The redhead takes the manhattan, sips, and says, "Thanks, but this is far too strong for me."

I put my free hand on her hip, pull her in and kiss her hard, tasting the whiskey fresh on her lips. And she lets me, for a moment, before pushing me away, laughing, spilling half of both our drinks soundlessly onto the wooden floor.

"A little presumptive?" she yells, wiping her half-smiling mouth.

"Life is short," I say, and look at my drink, regretting such waste of the good stuff.

"It's not *that* short," she says, walking past me.

I stroll over to the stage, think about heading backstage, but instead get on the stage, put my drink down and look down on the small crowd below me. I sway to the music and feel that they're all there for me. Dancing for me. Enjoying life because of me.

Then the floor below me populates with a mountain of dead, discolored bodies. A few left alive struggle underneath the mass to get free, call my name and ask for help, but I cannot move from the stage, cannot dive into that mess of rotting flesh to save anyone. Not now. Not then. Not ever.

Then the lights flicker and everyone dances. The redhead dances alone as Sanchez consoles his distraught date, a crowd of painted up flesh surrounds Gem, and Eric dances on their outskirts, arms pumping, yelling out "woot" and "biatches" too frequently.

I consider again going backstage, but feel I shouldn't. The song changes to Milli Vanilli's "Girl You Know It's True" and I hop from the stage, jump into the middle of the jitter-bugging crowd and start breakdancing, spinning on my back, twirling on my head, the music hall gravitating around me upside down, legs and feet gyrating the wrong way up, and my name shouted through laughter over and over and over and over.

I awake backstage on an old green couch in a little room with pale green walls. The paint's peeling, the linoleum floor's stained grey, and there's an empty cooler next to me. The pounding bass from the music hall, slightly muffled, still shakes the place. Eric wanders in and I projectile vomit all over his feet in the entranceway but he doesn't seem to notice.

"So this is where the stars hang before hitting the stage, huh?" he asks, sitting down in a dingy orange chair across from me and lighting up a joint.

I pull myself into a sitting position, put my head in my hands, and say, "No stars play here."

Eric chuckles, "Yeah, right. But I bet you're feeling right at home back here, famous poet that you are."

A bat that was sleeping in the corner of the room flutters awake and exits through the open door.

"Jesus fucking Christ," I say and search for my Winstons.

Then the redhead walks in.

"Hey, watch it with that kind of talk. I could be a Catholic school girl with virgin ears."

She collapses onto Eric's lap and they kiss, Eric handling her like too many fistfuls of spaghetti.

I get up, about to puke again, when Eric reaches over the redhead, pushes me back onto the couch, and says, "Hold on, hold on."

I hold on. The bile in my throat burning.

"This is Abigail," he says and I vomit hard against the wall, though they don't notice. I wipe my mouth, feel for any loose teeth, then wipe my hand on the green couch and shake her hand.

In taking my hand she gets up and takes a seat next to me. "You don't seem like a good person," she says, her blue eyes darkening.

"Excuse me?" I ask.

"There's something wrong with you."

"What makes you say that?" I say as Eric hands me a bottle of MGD. I take a sip.

"You don't like people."

"Which people?" I ask.

"All people."

"How do you know that?"

"I can see it in your face. In your eyes."

"Jesus," I say, looking at Eric. "Fucking hippies, right? Can't get away from them."

"You're full of hurt," Abigail says.

"And how the fuck do you know that?" I ask as I down half the beer. Eric smirks to himself and pulls out a bag of something.

"Just as I know that my name, Abigail, is your favorite among all names. It may help you keep the fantasy alive, Luke, but it's just a name. I also know you've got very little to be sorry for. Just as I know you blame the world for your own shortcomings. Just as I know you think yourself more important than you are because you never tried hard enough to be anything important. Just as I know you hate yourself for that. And just as I know you've been staring at me like a rabid dog all night long."

I exhale an enormous amount of air, surprised the walls don't come down, and look to my sudden and best ally, Eric, and say, "For fuck's sake. Can you believe this shit? Who is this girl? Who the fuck does she think she is?"

Eric stands up in the small, pale green room and takes a long drag from his joint, holds the smoke for a while, lets it out, and says, "She's your fucking *conscience*, man."

"Don't fuck with me," I say, grabbing the joint from him

and taking a drag, filling the room with green smoke. "I don't appreciate morons trying to philosophize with me."

Then a sudden vibration. Everything moving first to the left, then to the right, in herky-jerky motions over a sequence of five seconds, like a filmstrip fighting its way through a reluctant reel.

"Luke, quit kidding yourself," Abigail says, and looks away toward the exit leading to a hallway that leads back to the main room.

That exit that seemed a few feet away minutes ago stretches into miles before me.

"Who's kidding who?" I ask, stand up, and feel the earth yank me back to the couch.

"You're lost. You're sick. You're so sick it makes others sick. You need help, but you won't accept it. You think it's everyone else that has the problem. Don't you? You do. I can see that. Your sickness is so rooted, so old, you can't even tell it's yourself that's wrong. You're the problem. You're the *entire* problem. You're just deformed inside now. And you only begrudge others their happiness because you simply can't understand it. Right?"

She lights a long Marlboro and her face glows brighter than anything in the room. Green smoke lingers before her face. Then she very gently removes the joint from my hand, takes a drag from that and a pull from a bottle of wine she must have found beside the couch. She returns the joint me.

"I'm… Abigail, I don't think…" I manage to say, excited and confused at the brushing of her fingers against mine in the exchange.

Then, with silence between us all, I consider further and say, "I'm trying, Abigail."

Abigail crosses her legs, puts the Marlboro to her lips, sucks back the smoke and blows it out her nose, then looks at Eric who's lounging crossways in the chair, amused and dopey-eyed. She smiles at him sincerely and my heart snaps like an old floorboard under heavy feet.

I watch Abigail's beautifully pale face, crystal blue eyes, cascading red hair that radiates in the green light, and feel my throat slit open, blood gushing from my split neck. As I put a hand to it to stop the gushing I realize it's just the words stuck in my throat trying to get out.

I finish my beer, give Eric back the joint and he hands me a fresh MGD though I don't know where he's finding them. Then Tiffany's version of "I Think We're Alone Now" seeps into the room.

"You're a sad person, Luke," Abigail says. Sweet smells fill the room along with green clouds.

"No more sad than you or your pusher," I say, motioning toward Eric.

I half-laugh, which causes them both to laugh, seemingly, along with me, and before I know what's happening I've broken my beer bottle into a jagged handle, which goes through Abigail's ribcage far more easily than I would have thought, the sound and feel of it like puncturing stale cardboard, and the bottle pulls out even easier, so fast, in fact, that I slice open Eric's throat before he can gather what's happening, blood showering me from head to toe, the room going from green to brown.

With Eric collapsed in the same crosswise position in the chair and Abigail collapsed over the side of the couch and exsanguinating, I stand up, find Eric's secret stash of MGDs behind his chair, pop one open, sit back down next Abigail, and watch as she discolors the already discolored couch, watch as her pale, slightly flushed face goes blue.

I sip at the warming beer, feel the blood caking on me with each second as my stomach starts to turn over. I hold back the convulsion, though, not really needing to throw up now.

The bat that left the room earlier returns to its corner, a folded note clutched in its mouth. I'm unwilling to pull the thing from its tiny black mouth and read what's there.

Eric is blue. The walls are pale green and brown in splatters of drying blood. I weep profusely, convulse and dry heave, hold onto my own ribs as I bend forward, shaking.

Then I pull Abigail's body to my own and can feel the lightness of her bloodless figure, the frailness of it. I hold her to me, kiss her cold forehead, run my fingers through her blood-soaked hair and choke on my own sobbing, squeezing her tight as I yell, "I'm sorry! I said I was *trying*!" until my throat is sore and I can no longer hear the music from the other room over my own voice. "I'm sorry," I say again. "I'm sorry."

I apologize as many times as it takes and for as long as it takes.

I then leave the room with a clear conscience and re-enter the pulsing music hall where lights flicker, a warm hue blankets the vibrant gold and deep red motif, and the mangled few shimmy to a booming Color Me Badd song.

When Abigail and Eric exit backstage just after me, my heart sinks. My breathing stops. My feet turn to stone. I'm weighted down by a crippling embarrassment and an immense sadness and loneliness that hollows out my gut. And both of them refuse to even look me in the eye before re-joining the dance.

BRET EASTON ELLIS

We're at Borders at the Stonestown Mall surrounded by deadbeats, hippies, half-dead college students, fat, uncrippled men that wear catheter bags anyway and smell of moldy skin. A kind of old, rotted cabbage aroma wafts over the crowd seated in folding chairs in the all-too-bright space as Bret Easton Ellis reads about his fictional self in *Lunar Park* with a bit too much confidence, arrogance, and dramatic whimsy.

People mill about behind him with their lattes, wearing expensive suede jackets and face paint that says "Dickless" or "my other bike is an SUV" and they're stopping the frazzled-looking Borders employees and asking them where books on colon cancer or Oprah are and the employees keep wetting themselves but the customers nor Bret Easton Ellis notice.

Then Bret Easton Ellis takes off his black Wayfarers to accentuate a particularly poignant part of *Lunar Park* where he meets a character he invented grown into flesh and blood. He says, "Brilliant, right?" and smiles at us all and everyone erupts into a cacophony of clapping, whooping, and yelling, and two guys throw their tidy whities at him.

I stay silent, put my hand on Abigail's knee, feel its ice coldness. She smirks, then scoffs and pushes my hand away.

"But I love you, I say," I say, for effect.

She smirks again and says, "You're a cancer," then kisses me on the cheek and puts her hand on my dick and leaves it there as her face fills with tumors.

"I hate your fucking guts, she says," she says, for effect.

Bret Easton Ellis notices and keeps his eyes on us and I feel bad for Abigail that I'm unable to get hard because her face is full of tumors.

"Cancerous love," Bret Easton Ellis says, and then the entire audience turns around and stares at us.

The guy in face paint and the expensive suede jacket walks up to Bret Easton Ellis and asks him where the books on ass cancer are and Bret Easton Ellis directs him to children's books.

Everyone claps again and I cough up a feather even though yesterday all I could cough up was helium. The music overhead turns to gunfire, then lightning, then the exact last sounds of everyone that died of the plague 700 years ago remixed to a Daft Punk beat.

After the reading, Abigail wanders off to the café and I

walk up to Bret Easton Ellis as he gathers his things into a leather carrier bag—books, papers, pictures of tied-up people getting shit on while being read Nazi propaganda, pens, little bags of fingernail clippings, and magazines like *The Economist* and *Teen Beat.*

"*Lunar Park*," I say, standing before Bret Easton Ellis who is tall, balding, and pudgy-faced.

He smiles knowingly. "You like it? It's good, right? I felt like I really changed the way horror stories can be approached and that I pushed the boundaries of where fiction and nonfiction begin. Also, I'm pretty sure it'll be made into a movie."

"It's crap," I say. I put my hands in my pockets and Bret Easton Ellis's head goes in and out like bad TV reception, returns as Big Bird's head then Bella Lugosi's, then Big Bird's again, then back to Bret Easton Ellis's. Then back to Big Bird's.

"Oh," he says, seemingly reserved. "So you've read it?"

"Yeah."

"Well, it had moments, but I sort of knew I pulled that thing out of my ass. Even made plenty of references to the dog's ass in it. That's what they call *literary allusion.* I think that's what they call it, anyway. But I figured I could get away with it. And I did. Look," he says, holding up a paper coffee cup, "free coffee."

I hand over my copy and Bret Easton Ellis signs it, "To Luke, Go Fuck Yourself You Know-Nothing Cunt! Best, B.E.E." and adds a little smiley face after it.

I shake Bret Easton Ellis's hand, thank him and make my

way to the café to find Abigail where she's sitting at a table near the window that looks out onto Nordstrom's storefront and a parking lot that looks a lot like my face. She's reading an instructional book about dealing with friends and family that suffer from mental conditions such as sloth, greed, gluttony, lust, wrath, envy, and capitalism. I think there's a carpenter in it and a bunch of men that fuck their daughters up the ass. I think I read it once, but I'm not sure if that was before or after the stigmata.

My mouth fills with locusts but they're quick and exit before anyone notices.

Abigail looks up and her neon blue eyes, bordered by a dark blue eyeliner, shock me and turn me dumb. I reach out and touch her face, move a strand of red hair behind her ear, and tell her that I love her. She pushes my hand away, laughs nervously, looks around, and tells me to stop, says that I'm speaking nonsense. I ask her to come out with me to the parking lot that looks like my face. To fuck me on it. To make love to me surrounded by cold glistening metal vehicles that when put together on cold black asphalt look just like my face, but she says no and that she doesn't think the parking lot looks very much like my face anyway and I disagree and feel like she just took something away from me.

"I'm sorry I murdered you," I say.

She looks up at me.

"I'm sorry I gutted you like a fish. You're not a fish. I know you're not," and then I remove the hook in her mouth and she smiles, says thank you, and calls me crazy.

"And I'm sorry I killed your boyfriend—that I slit open his throat like a strung up pig and liked it when he squealed like one even though I know he'd never fry up good and go well with eggs and hash browns."

"That reminds me," Abigail says, searching through her dark red velvet purse as I stand over her at her small table in the café at Borders. "I need to call Eric."

"Um, why?"

"His mother died," she says, then laughs.

I can only think about Abigail naked, wet, and screaming until her face melts off, falls into her lap and gets pushed away like a smoldering soup that's left her mid-section warped and violent like a modernist painting. I want to put my face into it and let it get warped and violent like a modernist painting.

Instead, I have no patience, so I walk away to find self-help books that can tell me how to kill someone better and pleasure oneself afterward, and from there on out be pleasured and fulfilled by life.

While walking through the fluorescent-lit space filled with yuppies, cripples, deaf and dumb people, illiterates, the homeless, and large bi-pedal crickets raping the checkout clerks, I recall that I used to work here. That it was my first real job I had in the city. That I used to organize these shelves with poetry and Oprah's books and books on ass cancer and that when asked by a customer where he could find a book about helping a friend with colon cancer that I directed him to the correct section while nearly crying from holding back a fit of laughter, having gone mad from answering such questions day in and day out while stationed at the info desk, and how holding back that fit of laughter tore muscles in my abdomen and chest and had me out of work for over a week without pay.

I remember lying in bed, hardly able to move, watching *Gilligan's Island* and Sally Jessie Rafael scalp another Native American while feeding myself only on the pigeons that flew through my window who tried to entertain me with stories of the talking bugs that were their friends. Then I would remove their heads and end their crazy talk, suck down their blood so I could rehydrate, pluck their wings, remove their fleas, spit out the gristle, and chew for hours on their fat to get me through the recuperation.

Just so I could get back as quickly as possible to shelving books about Oprah and ass cancer at Borders.

While in a daze and about to throw up I bump into Bret Easton Ellis who's going through his own books on the shelves in the fiction section with a pen, signing them with winking smiley faces and crossing out words within each book such as "that" and "were" and replacing them with "cunt" and "cockface" while laughing and scratching his Big Bird beak with self-congratulations.

"You have lots of money," I say.

He looks up from scribbling in a paperback copy of *Less*

Than Zero, and says, “Um, yeah?”

“You should get on Rogaine or something,” I say, then grab his copy of *Less Than Zero* away from him and then take his pen, too, and begin replacing words like “disappear” with “kill someone” and others like “Ray-Bans” with “dead baby seals”.

I hand it back to him and pick up a book about Mount Everest that starts with the accomplishments of all that conquered it and ends with a high resolution photo collage of those that died on it, frozen in their places, their grey faces glowing amidst their neon snow gear. Just left there because going there to get them and bring them back would be too dangerous and costly. Though how someone can get there to take pictures of a frozen face clutched in pain and why they can’t be brought back is never answered.

Next I know, me and Bret Easton Ellis are at the Olive Garden in the mall and he’s telling me not to order anything but booze while bossing around the wait staff to bring us more and more free breadsticks and the breadsticks are easily the best thing I’ve ever eaten.

Bret Easton Ellis drinks mojito after mojito even though it’s technically winter, and I sip a vodka martini while he slowly bleeds out our waitress over the table and pays off the hostess to look the other way, calls it research, says he’s doing a study for a script treatment, that his actions are necessary to make more books that can be made into bad movies that will make him more money than the books and everyone smiles and asks for his autograph, and so I take their napkins and copies of *The Rules of Attraction* and sign them with, "I wrote this fucking book, bitch, don't you ever ask Bret Easton Ellis to sign a book he didn't even write ever again," and then finish it off with a heart that looks like the Smashing Pumpkins' heart but with my initials in it.

After ditching out on the bill at the Olive Garden I remember that I also worked there, that I spilled beer on customers, dropped trays of food all over the dining room, and learned how to make a shitty wine sound exotic while working on getting blowjobs during my shifts from out-of-town women 20 years my senior. Then I remember that after three weeks of it—and deciding blowjobs from old women didn't suffice—that I took my notepad and apron back to the manager's office after a shift and tied him up, the ropes cutting into his fat wrists, ankles, and neck, bruises breaking out there along with blood clusters as I cut up the apron and notepad and the $14 in tips I made that day and fed it to him, forcing it down his throat with the cheap blush wine they made me peddle with an Italian accent. Then I told him that I quit.

"What happened to the redhead?" Bret Easton Ellis asks as we're standing in front of Mrs. Fields where Robin Williams orders a chocolate chip cookie five-feet in diameter that reads, "Happy Anniversary, I've Never Been So Depressed," and everyone that sees it laughs and he cries and tells them how he gave out PlayStations for Halloween. His furry body becomes coated in tears. His skin cries. Then he turns away from the counter, says, "Oh, hello, Bret," and scurries on by. I try to stop him to tell him that I thought *Toys* was a brilliant movie, despite what stuck-up pricks say, but he'd already rolled into a furry little ball and bounced down the escalator.

"What redhead?" I ask, chomping into a doughy peanut butter cookie.

"The one you were with at my reading," Bret Easton Ellis says before biting into a chocolate chocolate-chip cookie.

"Oh, she's telling her dead boyfriend that his mother's dead," I say and throw the last half of my cookie at a kid in a Hot Dog on a Stick uniform. "Or, maybe she's trying to get back with him. The language people use today—I don't understand most of it."

"Me either," Bret Easton Ellis says. "That's why I can't write good books anymore."

For a moment I think that maybe I also worked at Mrs. Field's but then realize I've never had a job that good.

"I'll call her," I tell Bret Easton Ellis and he looks pleased.

Abigail says that even though I murdered her and her boyfriend, she'd be pleased to join me and Bret Easton Ellis at the Mrs. Field's, especially if she could bring Eric, which I said was out of the question but she shows up with Eric anyway and he seems overly excited about the cookies and tells me before saying hello that he'll probably get a dozen for his mom.

"I'm Bret Easton Ellis," Bret Easton Ellis says, shaking

Eric's hand. Then he takes Abigail's hand and kisses it, then he takes back Eric's hand and kisses it, then he puts his Wayfarers on and pretends to be cool and takes a seat by himself at a table overlooking the first floor of the mall.

"I like him," Abigail says.

Eric goes up to the counter and orders a dozen mud-flavored cookies for his mom.

"Why'd you bring him?" I ask Abigail.

"Who, Eric?"

"Yeah."

"He's my boyfriend. You know that, Luke. You're lucky he's not the jealous type or we'd never get to hang out."

"Are you serious?" I ask as Bret Easton Ellis lowers his Wayfarers down the bridge of his nose, stares at us, winks, and smiles.

Somewhere in the distance Robin Williams either laughs or cries like a sad or happy coyote.

Frustrated, I look back at Eric, then to Bret Easton Ellis, then back at Abigail, and all I want to do is kiss her wet, red mouth, rip her face from her skull and wear it around for a year.

"Luke, you knew this wasn't a date, right?" Abigail asks, all seriousness and composure.

"Everyone that climbs Mount Everest climbs over the bodies of those that died before them, bodies just left there because the climb is so hard that taking the dead home with them is not an option," I say.

"That's beautiful, Luke. See, that's why I like hanging out with you. You can be so difficult sometimes, but sometimes you say the most beautiful things."

"You're crazy, I say," I say for effect.

She laughs and blushes.

Eric, holding a box of cookies wrapped in a pink bow, joins us and takes Abigail's hand.

"Hey, Luke," he says, having a hard time looking me in the eyes.

I walk over to Bret Easton Ellis and sit across from him, don't say anything for a very long time, think I see Cameron below throwing her child into a deep well, then realize it's just some dark haired woman I don't know throwing a child into a deep well.

Bret Easton Ellis pulls a flask from his suit jacket pocket, takes off his Ray-Bans, and drinks from it, then leans forward with sudden fervor and says, "You. You want advice."

"I do?"

"You want to know, 'why'?"

"Why what?"

"You want to feel confident. To know what it's like to know what you're doing in this labyrinth. To know how to follow it without hurting anyone or getting lost. To feel like if you ran into David Bowie or a troll you'd know exactly what to say. And if you happened to be chasing a redhead through there with a face full of cancer, you'd like to know how to catch her and cure it. You want to know what it feels like to know that you know what you want and that what you want is to help others, to be there for them, to stop the bleeding after you've cut them."

"What are you talking about?"

"I don't know," Bret Easton Ellis says and takes another pull from his flask, puts it away, sighs, and puts the sunglasses back on.

"I'm not Clay," I say.

"I know. I know," Bret Easton Ellis says. "I just…." He stares off, goes distant. He tears up behind the Wayfarers, I imagine.

"It's not like this," Bret Easton Ellis continues. "In the desert. It's full of less. Full of less of *this*. And, Blair—I mean, whatever your name is—I don't know what I'm saying half the time. I just want to drag you back to my room, tie you up, and waterboard you while I read every word Ronald Reagan ever wrote down out loud until you understand what that man really said and what that man really wanted, because, you fucking kids—you goddamned kids, I don't think any of you *get* it. You just don't get it! What Ronald Reagan wanted was for me to rape you! He was a *good* man."

"I can't remember anything about him," I say. "I think my grandmother voted for him. If women could vote back then. I can't remember."

Bret Easton Ellis looks frustrated and frazzled so I leave him, walk over to Abigail and Luke who stare into each other's eyes like mentally handicapped children incapable of speech.

"Oh. Hi, Luke," Eric says, not looking up at me. He's got something in his hands and he's holding Abigail's left hand.

"Hi, Luke," Abigail says, not looking away from Eric.

The soundtrack from *Labyrinth* starts playing overhead, but then I realize it's just Bret Easton Ellis behind us singing to himself the hit song from the movie, "As the World Falls Down".

"We just got engaged, Luke!" Eric says, finally looking up at me, his eyes glossy, lost, and dumb.

"He just proposed," Abigail says, her eyes wet. Then she shows me a ring with an impossibly small diamond embedded in what looks like a small rabbit's still-beating heart. Blood runs down her wrist, stops at the elbow, and drips onto the table.

"In front of Mrs. Field's?" I ask.

They don't say anything, just grab each other across the table and start making out in a mess of two faces seeming to have a hard time finding the other's mouth.

I look back at Bret Easton Ellis. He's looking away from us still singing the song from *Labyrinth*.

Next thing I know, we're all on MUNI heading north on 19th Avenue because Bret Easton Ellis says he wants to take the lucky couple to Golden Gate Park and toast to their nuptials with the finest champagne.

I tell Bret Easton Ellis there's no champagne in Golden

Gate Park. That, in fact, there's nothing at all to do at Golden Gate Park. That this isn't New York and he should snap out of it.

He just looks at me, smiles through the Wayfarers, shows me the bleached blue-white smile of Hollywood success.

"Don't you have a car?" I ask Bret Easton Ellis as the bus hits pothole after pothole after homeless person, making the trip bumpy and arduous.

"Um," he says, shoulders slumped, staring out the window. "I think I left it in Lunar Park."

"That's not a place," I say. "That's your crappy book."

"Yeah," he says quietly, staring at his reflection in the window.

In the seats behind us either Eric is fingering Abigail or Abigail is fingering Eric so I keep my eyes forward until we reach Lincoln Way and deboard.

"Get down from there!" Eric yells, laughing, holding a bottle of Dom Pérignon 1966 that Bret Easton Ellis had delivered via helicopter. The helicopter landed in an ocean of light and wind at the polo field and took off before the cops could be alerted. They left us with a half dozen bottles and took off north scaring the bison at the bison field in the park maintained by vegetarians that raise bison in order to sacrifice them to their vegetarian god.

"I'm going to jump!" Bret Easton Ellis says, standing on the roof of what must be an equipment shed for the park rangers. No higher than 12 feet.

"I'll fucking do it, you fucking snot-nosed know-nothing shits!" Then he takes a drink from his bottle of Dom Pérignon 1966, tries to pull his pants down to moon us, and falls.

"Oh, shit!" Eric yells.

Abigail makes small animal sounds.

I stand back with my bottle of Dom Pérignon 1966 and make sure the last two bottles remain guarded.

In the barely lit darkness, Eric helps Bret Easton Ellis get his pants back on. "There ya go, man," Eric says, getting him to his feet, Bret Easton Ellis's arms now around both Eric and Abigail as they help walk him to the side of this manmade lake where yuppies play with their remote-controlled yachts before making the mayor go down on them on their full-sized yachts out in the bay.

All three of them sit quietly on the bench, staring at the moon's reflection on the manmade lake until Bret Easton Ellis looks back at me and asks, half-heartedly, "Hey, whatsyourname, is there any more champagne left? I broke mine in the fall. I mean, my bottle. I broke my bottle."

"Um, yeah. No problem. There's one left, I think," I say as I swallow what's left of mine, grab one of the last for Bret Easton Ellis and pop the other one open for myself, aiming the cork at Eric's head but missing miserably because of the darkness.

"So," Bret Easton Ellis says. "You two are getting married. That's fucking wonderful," he says, sitting between them and clinking their bottles. "I can't say—I can't begin to tell you how much respect and envy I have for the sanctity of marriage. If only I could ever…."

"That's really nice, Bret," Abigail, says. "Thanks."

"You're welcome, red—"

"Oh? Do you like my hair? It's—"

"Uh, yeah, sure, red. As I was saying. Marriage is beautiful. And I have nothing but the highest level of respect and romantic awe when two people get together and decide to make a three-year commitment to each other. It's truly beautiful."

Then Bret Easton Ellis spills half his bottle over the couple's heads before running off to the edge of the lake, laughing like a drugged hyena, and dropping his pants to moon us. Then, straightening himself up, pants still around the ankles, he takes the champagne bottle in hand and drinks while pissing into the lake.

Walking up behind Eric and Abigail I say, "Can I talk to you?"

"Sure, Luke, what's up?" Eric asks.

"Not you, shitbreath."

"Luke," Abigail says, straining the Dom Pérignon 1966 from her hair. "It's not a good time, obviously."

"But we need to—"

"Luke, stop it."

Abigail gets up from the bench, shakes the last of the champagne from her hair, pushes it off her clothes, from her exposed skin, and I just want to lick it from her, savor it and set her afire, watch her body turn to ash and agony.

Next I know, the sound of waves gets louder because we're walking west through the dark thicket of the park and Bret Easton Ellis is ahead of me walking between Eric and Abigail, their hands in his, and I realize we're strolling through the public golf course where I used to come with my college roommates, hauling a 12-pack of Keystone Ice and two packs of Winston Lights and a few irons with which I used to smack the shit out of golf balls, get frustrated and beat my friends until they agreed to never challenge me again. And how they remained true to me, for a time, whether or not the blood washed off.

Just before we get to the Great Highway at the park's western edge, Bret Easton Ellis, Eric, and Abigail, hand-in-hand, veer off into the trees and blackness. I continue on over through the trees and blackness and cross the Great Highway, nearly get hit by a silver car with its headlights off, and walk over to Ocean Beach, which is windy, cold, and full of rats sprinting out from beneath patches of thick crab grass.

The Pacific goes meek beneath cold air and moonlight lighting up its crests and whitewater, then just licks lamely at the shore and bores me. Bonfires show tongues of orange up and down the beach where college kids wipe the snot from their noses and drink some of the first beers they've ever had while feeling inclined to share their Bud Light with the mental patient that won't leave their fireside who keeps laughing and saying "Up your asses!" after every drink.

I walk up to the edge of the water glimmering in a neon-blue that almost isn't and feel a hand on my shoulder.

"I'm gonna go now," Bret Easton Ellis says, then he removes his hand from my shoulder to clear some blood and grey matter from his mouth.

"Oh?"

"Yeah. I gotta go. I wish I could say this was fun. I wish…." He looks away from me down toward the Cliff House up the beach and wipes sand or tears from his eyes.

"Yeah, well, okay. No problem," I say.

Bret Easton Ellis walks into the ocean, first taking off his suit jacket, then his shoes and pants, then everything else. Blue-lit and bare-assed, he walks all the way into the dark sea until I can see nothing left of him. And it's just quiet around me except for a mild wind and the crackle of old wood giving up to the bonfires.

Then I hear, "Hey, Luke!" as Abigail approaches, a comically large smile on her face as she pulls the shoulder of her sweater in place and adjusts her bra beneath it. I think I see Eric across the way trying to cross the highway while pulling on his pants. I keep praying to god that he trips and falls under the wheel of some expensive sports car, but he manages his way across, bumbling and fumbling, until he's standing before us with a vacant look and dumb smile.

I pull Abigail aside by the elbow and say, "Listen, Abigail, I just watched Bret Easton Ellis walk himself, naked, into the ocean and disappear."

"Luke?" she says, still smiling and adjusting her clothing. "What are you talking about?"

"Abigail—"

"Who's Abigail?" Abigail asks, finally done getting her clothes all settled.

The ocean blushes for a split second as I picture her naked and tied to a Christmas tree wrapped in a ribbon bearing my name while she gives birth to our first child still tethered to her via a tinsel umbilical cord.

"You, Abigail. You're Abigail." I let go of her elbow and she drifts.

"Luke, are you still talking about that friend of yours that died?"

"What? Abigail, what are you—"

"I'm sorry," she says, tears welling up. "But some of the things you say! I mean, I can't even completely believe you about this friend of yours. Abigail was her name? Really? Are you sure? I mean, I just can't. You're so difficult. It wouldn't be too unlike you to make something like that up, would it? Would it?"

"Abigail, why are you talking like this? I would never make shit like that up. Why would you—"

"No, Luke. Seriously, stop it. This is sick."

"Abigail, your hair. It's so red. It's so red. I loved your hair first. It caught my eye before anything else. It's like gilded blood continuously flowing from your pale, your beautifully pale scalp. It's what first caught my eye before I realized that I loved you completely."

"Luke, I just dyed my hair red, like, yesterday. This is too weird. I have to go. I have to get back to my kid."

"Your kid?"

"Yeah, shit for brains. Toby. I have to get back to him. I don't know why I let you drag me and Eric out here this late at night. The sitter's gonna have a fit. I'm a bad mom."

"Mom?"

"Yeah, I'm a shitty mom for hanging out with nutjobs like you." Then she turns away from me. "Eric, can we just—can we just go now?" she asks, picking up a shoe she lost in the sand.

"Sure, honey. Yeah, no problem," Eric says, putting his arm around Abigail's middle and giving me a look of confusion. Like, he feels bad for me but can't do anything to help.

They walk up to the sand-strewn parking lot and get into Eric's red '94 Mustang and pull away into the night.

The moon bobs above the distant ocean horizon like a child's luminescent balloon, and the wind kicks sand in my face as bonfire after bonfire up and down the beach goes out one by one along with each and every star in the sky.

"Abigail? I ask," I ask for effect, then turn my back on the Pacific and feel it nibble at my heels and continue its efforts to bore me.

MMBURR

PART I

Mmburr. Burrmmm. Mmburr. Burrmmm. Syd's pushing the second of two 20s Wilson gave her into the little booth's cash machine, which doesn't seem to want his money. He handed those 20s off to her, told her it's my birthday and that she should do something special for me. She said she would and brought me back here to a long hallway of little booths, each red-lit by moaning TVs.

As Syd continues her efforts to slip the 20 into the machine, I work at slipping the black latex condom that she handed me over my half-erect dick. I encircle the hard ring of the condom with my thumb and forefinger and try to slide it down, but I'm not hard enough and it doesn't work. The suction sounds from my bare ass and thighs moving on the sticky red vinyl bench-seat keep distracting me as does Syd's palpable impatience with the machine's uncooperative behavior.

"Derrick will be in here telling you to get the fuck out before I can get this damned money into this piece of shit," Syd says, looking back at me, exasperated, her dark hair falling in front of her eyes, which are already hidden behind the black-rimmed reading glasses she has worn all night, even while on stage.

As she kneels before that machine I finally notice she's wearing a very revealing black bikini and can't get the idea out of my mind that she's about to shimmy up a palm tree for a coconut.

Syd's skin illuminates from the screen above the cash machine that's showing a brunette eating a blonde's pussy while getting pounded relentlessly from behind by the same bear that modeled for the California state flag many years ago. She keeps yelling, "I'm coming! Oh, God, I'm coming!" The other woman, while pulling the brunette's mouth back down onto her cunt, yells, "Get… his… autograph!"

"Um, who's Derrick?" I ask, not looking away from the job at hand of getting this rubber onto my increasingly limp cock.

"Ugh…. The bodyguard. If anyone's in here for more than eight minutes, he comes looking to make sure everything's OK," she says, then adds, "Finally!" as the bill slithers into the slim slot, quieting the machine.

"I only get eight minutes?" I ask, tongue now sticking out of the side of my mouth, concentrating real hard on getting hard and getting this black piece of latex securely sheathed around my pathetic excuse for manhood.

On her knees, she swivels away from the glowing screen and cash machine and shuffles toward me, placing her hands on my exposed thighs that shine like two thick pieces of Ivory soap in the light of porno.

"That's all you'll nee—" she says, stopping herself the second her hand wraps around my softened dick. "Jesus, you're not even hard?" she asks, annoyed, then adjusts her attitude and purrs and moves her head down like a heavy wave over my dick, mouthing the black piece of rubber down my scared and nervous penis. In the undulating motion toward my flaccid appendage she also managed to expertly discard her bikini top. Her hard nipples now mock my cock as they sift and brush against my knees and give me goosebumps.

My heart pounds, but none of the blood it's pumping goes to the right place. I turn my attention away from Syd's black head of hair bobbing back and forth over my lap and watch the porno on the screen. By now the scene's over but the camera hasn't cut away and it shows the brown bear wiping his midsection briskly with a towel as the blonde and the brunette, now in robes, sit at a table laying out cards. After a thorough scrubbing, the brown bear drops his towel and sits and takes his cards. "Go Fish," he says and the two women first study their own cards and look perplexed. One frowns. One smiles.

I grimace. The scene makes me nauseous for some reason and that doesn't help my current situation.

"Derrick's going to be in here any minute," Syd says, pulling her face up off my plastic-covered cock, her mouth wet-rimmed with effort.

"It's OK," I say, touching her shoulder gently and pushing her away. "Just sit back there and let me look at you."

"Do you want me to do anything?" she asks, kneeling back, pushing her hair away and back behind her pale shoulders before playing with her dark nipples and starring me in the eyes, the TV screen reflected in her glasses.

"Tell me again how much you love reading," I say, stroking my completely limp cock. "Tell me how much you love Vonnegut," I say, pretending to grunt and enjoy myself.

She had intrigued me earlier in the night (or was it a year ago?) after she straddled me and gyrated atop me to "Tonight, Tonight" by The Smashing Pumpkins. Afterward, she asked what I did and I told her I'm a writer. She said she was, too. She said she loved Vonnegut and was in school to be a writer, herself. I told her to leave school and marry me and she laughed. I told her I'd write poems about her and she laughed. I told her I'd make lots of money and take care of her and she laughed even harder.

I guessed she must be going to a better school than the one I had almost graduated from.

"Oh, wait," she says, pulling her fingers away from plucking her nipples to reach inside her bikini bottom. She pretends that the mere touch is pleasurable, groaning just a bit as her fingers slip down around her pussy lips. "There was something else," she continues, "that I was supposed to give you."

Her hand withdraws from between her legs. She puts that hand in front of her face and licks it from palm to the tip of her fingers. Leaning forward, she grabs me behind the neck and pulls me toward her and kisses me deeply, her long, wet, strong tongue pushing the powdery pill into the back of my throat. I pull back, gagging, and she pulls back, again, laughing. The grunts and groans and damp slapping sounds from the porno act as the requisite laugh track.

"What the fuck was that?" I ask, leaning over as my sinuses suddenly open and the medicine-bitter flavor syrups down my esophagus.

"Just a little birthday gift," Syd says and begins to mouth my half-erect dick again.

I lean back and hit my head against the cheap plasterboard of the red-lit booth. I can't stop thinking about the way my legs are sticking to the vinyl seat and can't stop wondering why that reminds me of my aunt's station wagon with the wood paneling on the side. I can't stop thinking of how me and my cousins, Tammy and Erin, would ride in that station wagon whenever they came down from Oregon to visit and how we'd make faces at the passing drivers and laugh whenever we distracted one of them enough to swerve off the road, crash into a barrier, and go careening through the windshield like a heavy-headed bird—that and how the light was soft and the freeway was a pale grey and felt like a place for getting somewhere. Somewhere like Hollywood or Winnipeg.

As Syd's hard nipples grate across my kneecaps, I can't help but wonder how everything used to be rounded on the edges. As a kid, and even through parts of your teenage years, you could bang your head right against anything and come away with only a tiny bruise. That bruise may stick around forever, it may even grow in size with time, but now if you go around and barely bump into something you lose a finger, an arm, a left nut. It used to be different, right? Not like this where you sink into the broken skin of a vinyl seat covered in weeks-old spunk and sweat and spit.

Then I feel the warmth of the pill blossoming in my stomach. The red room goes yellow around the edges, and soft.

For a second I just want to curl up and go to sleep, but my cock is finally hard now in Syd's literate mouth and I'm sure she's smiling through the mouthful. I smile, too, feeling loopy and happy for the first time in weeks, months. I lean a bit over Syd and reach into the pants-pocket of the jeans down around my ankles and palm a small pocket knife I'd forgotten to give back to a friend a long time ago. Leaning back I let Syd work my knob with expertise, then pop the small blade out with a click that gets lost in sounds of slurps and moans and a hallway of lonely orgasms.

With the knife next to her face, Syd finally removes her mouth with a smacking sound and looks up at me with big, confused eyes.

"Luke, what's this about?" she asks, wiping her mouth with the back of her glowing forearm.

I twirl the pocket knife in my hand, still smiling like a dope, happy as shit and completely forgetful of what I'm doing.

"Derrick will rip your fucking head off in a second if I tell him to. All I have to do is scream…. And I can scream real loud, Luke."

But she doesn't seem scared at all. She knows me. Yeah, she knows me.

"What…? *This*?" I ask, now holding the knife before my own face, as if I'd never seen it before in my life. "Oh… no, no…. No, this isn't for you, Syd. This is for *me*!"

"Huh?" she says, just confused.

"How much time do I have left?"

"Um," she turns her gaze to the screen and for the first time I notice there's a timer counting down in its bottom left-hand corner. It says I have 90 seconds.

"Here," I tell Syd, grabbing her left hand and pushing the knife into her grasp. "Cut me."

"Cut you? Are you crazy?"

"Do I look crazy to you?" I ask, grinning, and drooling, too, maybe.

Pulling her knife-hand toward me, I guide it to the inside of my thigh, just below my testicles.

I have 60 seconds left.

The drug in my system sent tiny little fireflies swarming beneath ever skin cell. I just want to cut them out so they can be free and I can tell them how much I love them for loving me. For giving me that warm feeling within that never comes anymore unless they visit.

"Here. Syd. Cut me… cut me right here." I take her right hand and get her to wrap her fingers round the base of my black-condom-covered shaft. "Just hold me there… and… and cut me."

I have 45 seconds left.

"Luke… I…." Syd says, but then pushes the knife into the hard, dehydrated muscle of my inner thigh and I convulse and yell and grab the back of her head just so I can feel the softness of her hair as I shoot my load into the condom's reservoir tip with two, three, four, five blissfully painful squirts.

Immediately Syd stands up, grabs her robe and slips it on. The pocket knife drops to the floor.

"I… I shouldn't have done that," she says, shaking her head before gliding through the heavy curtains covering the booth's slim entryway, leaving me alone with a bagful of come, a bleeding thigh, and an even stickier vinyl bench-seat.

I have 15 seconds left.

For a time I just sit back, my cock limp, and listen to the sounds of bodies slamming together, the sound of warm wet. On the screen now is Leatherface, and he's sliding teenagers onto big, hanging meat hooks. I smile and think that's weird but whatever floats your boat, I guess. Then I realize it isn't Leatherface but my uncle who was never in the station wagon with the wood paneling on the side. And one of the bodies he's hanging on hooks isn't a teenager at all, but my five-year-old brother, Sammy. Sammy's writhing on the hook, bawling and calling my name, screaming out for help. Shocked by the sight, I jump up and the black bag of come falls from me to the floor and leaks a pearly red fluid.

Shuffling toward the screen, my pants shackling my ankles, I place both hands on the slimy, tacky screen.

I have 10 seconds left.

"Sammy… hey, hey, Sammy. It's me, little pigeon. It's Luke. I'm here, guy. I'm here. Tell me what to do."

And it is Sammy, the little pigeon—a nickname I'd given him because he had small round eyes and a head the shape of a bird's and he often walked around like a sick pigeon. In a blink, Sammy's the only one on a hook surrounded by dozens of other serpentining hooks on chains clinking a metallic music that sounds like winter. It sounds like the chain link fence in the backyard that was open and rattling back and forth in a January gale when Sammy went missing 15 years ago. The backyard only lead to an alley lined with garages and dumpsters. Mom and dad weren't too worried, but they always pretended Sammy's mental and physical problems weren't actual handicaps.

"He'll be back," Mom said. "He's just off playing make-believe with his imaginary friends." Then she would return to crocheting another three-armed sweater for the little guy. It was hours before dad was home from work and the after-work bar, and dad wasn't worried either. "Sammy's a wanderer," dad said with lighter-fluid breath. "He just likes to wander. Like his old man," and he winked at me and grabbed my mom's knee and squeezed hard and winked at her and her face flushed for some reason and it all made me feel pretty sick. So I pretended to worry, since neither of them would, even though I was glad he was gone. I hoped he'd never come back and I'd never been gladder in my life. Sammy was a monster and an embarrassment. I never wanted a brother, anyway! I was shouting at them, but only in my head. I never wanted anything or anyone or anything! I would shout into my pillow later that night when Sammy still hadn't returned and my parents refused to call the police. I never wanted a brother! I shouted again and again into my salty, wet pillow, the wind rattling that gate again and again out back because we were leaving it unlocked for Sammy. I never wanted a brother!

I have 5 seconds left.

"I never wanted a brother!" I shout at the screen, unsticking my palms from it with a crackling noise, the image on the screen flashing on and off, then rippling. "I never wanted a brother!" I scream again, tears flowing from the yellow edges of my vision and running into my mouth where they taste like gutted insects.

Pulling my pants up, I shout once more at the screen,

and Sammy, on the hook, looks me dead in the eyes and says, "Luke, you sad sack of shit. You never had a brother," and I blunder out of the booth through the thick red curtains into the darkened hallway, still zipping up my fly and adjusting my belt.

Time's up.

PART II

Overhead, dim fluorescent lighting flickers. And then I realize: Silence. Absolute silence. No moans, no groans, no skin sticking to grimy vinyl, and no sounds of machines choking on money.

A gust corkscrews through the narrow hallway, ghosting the curtains covering each booth, and the hallway lengthens, grows for miles as the gust washes down it.

In that endless corridor, I steady myself, placing a hand against the black wall with my feet suctioned to the tacky concrete floor, also painted black. The booths are all made from cheap plywood and painted black, badly. The dark red curtains offer the only color in the wavering fluorescent light.

"Syd?" I yell. Then, less assuredly, "Um, Derrick?"

A small thump and groan and the curtains to a booth 60 feet away billow just a bit.

"Sammy?" I say, walking toward the stall with one hand still on the wall, feeling the room askew, slightly tilted, and afraid to lose my balance.

At the booth I hear a whisper ejaculate my name and the curtains once again flutter.

"Sammy?" I ask again and slowly part the curtains, revealing a small room, slightly bigger than the booth I was in with Syd. There's a large, square window at the back. It's covered by red velvet curtains on the opposite side of the glass. There's a standing lamp in the corner. In front of the window is a chair and a parking meter with instructions: 15 SECONDS FOR A QUARTER.

The warmth from the drug a little earlier starts to liquefy my limbs again and I realize I need a seat anyway, so I sit and dig my fingers into my change-pocket and pull out a quarter, which I quickly deposit into the meter, twisting the lever.

TICK-TICK-TICK!

Deafening sounds of clock hands flood the room forcing me to cover my ears and the curtain splits at the middle and recedes, revealing a blurry couple on a heart-shaped bed banging away, doggy-style. They're only a few feet behind the glass when I realize who the couple is.

TICK-TICK-TICK!

"Mom? Dad?" I say, my eyes clearing up from the drugs and earlier tears and present confusion. Just as I say it, however, the curtains close. I know I shouldn't but I have to know what the fuck's going on so I push another quarter into the meter and sure enough it's my mom and dad going to town on each. Dad's bald, his head shaved and glittery with sweat. His beer belly's swishing this way and that. Sweat drips from his grey goatee. Mom's beneath him, her hair a nasty tangle of spider webs and her floppy breasts flinging this way and that. She keeps slapping dad really fucking hard like she's trying to truly hurt him and dad laughs and as I stand and back away from the window I stumble over the chair that I just knocked over.

"Hey, Lukey! Luke, son! Get back here, boy!" I hear my dad yell, but I'm trying to get the fuck out of there, unwilling to believe my eyes, but not really fearing for my sanity as I know I'm on something, I just don't know what.

But, when I get to where the exit curtains should have been, there's a door, and it's locked. I slam into the door, both my mom and dad yelling my name and laughing and giggling like shitfaced teenagers, laughing so hard they're covering their mouths while still going at the deed.

TICK-TICK-TICK!

The door won't give, however, and I turn back to the window and notice the parking meter there has new instructions: ONE QUARTER TO CLOSE CURTAINS—15 SECONDS.

I don't even have to think about it, before I know it I'm at the meter with a handful of quarters, feeding the meter as fast as I can, but the curtain keeps closing and opening, proving I'm not feeding it fast enough, that someone has apparently pressed the remote control button on me: SLOW MOTION.

"What's the matter, Lukey?" my mom's saying, now on top of dad, the two of them a mass of loose and floppy and sweaty flesh. "We're making you a new brother!"

The curtain closes.

The curtain opens.

The curtain closes.

The curtain opens. Mom's on her back on the bed, her belly suddenly huge and stretched, and dad's standing at the foot of the bed, clapping his hands, hopping, and hooting. "Come on, boy! Come on, Sammy, you can do it! Crawl right out of that cunt, now, you squirmy little shit!" he yells and mom's screaming away, her head snapping left and right, spit and perspiration flying from her face. And before the curtain closes, dad's shoving a hand up mom, blood pulsing out onto the white sheets of the heart-shaped bed. "Alright, then, if you're not coming out, I'm coming to get you," dad yells.

Fast as I can, shoveling quarters into the meter, but my efforts are proving pointless and the curtain keeps slipping back and revealing more blood and wild faces and both my mom and dad screaming and yelling and grinding their teeth. Finally the curtain opens and stays open and there's my mom, seemingly unconscious, the room covered completely in a viscous red, and dad's between her legs with what looks like a bone saw, carving into her.

I put a hand to my mouth, but not quickly enough, and the vomit squirts between my fingers and sprays the glass with flecks.

"Don't worry, Lukey, we're getting you a new brother.

Don't you worry, we'll get your brother back," and I hear the cracking and splitting and a gushing sound and I close my eyes and when I open them dad is pressed up against the glass, covered in blood and mucus, yelling, suddenly soundless, but, in his right hand he holds a tiny, naked, three-armed, two-legged figure by the ankle. Dad's breathing hard against the glass, his breath fogging it. He's mouthing the words "I'm sorry" over and over again and lights are flicking on and off and I now realize the glass is not fogging before the tiny figure's quiet mouth as it is in front of my dad's.

Without thinking, I back away from the monstrosity at the window and fall back through the curtains, back out into the hallway, finally.

The lights out here go in and out. Black walls and floor. Curtains the color of browning blood. All still and quiet but for the sound of my shoe-soles getting sucked off by the soiled concrete floor. I wipe the vomit from my hands onto my jeans and hold back another gut-convulsion.

"Syd! Syd, goddammit!" I yell almost ripping out my eyeballs with spastic fingers. "Where the fuck did you go? Why did you leave me?"

It occurs to me then that the drugs couldn't have come from Syd. Why would she waste drugs on me? Wilson must have given them to her to give to me, along with the $40 he gave her to blow me. And it was Wilson's idea to come here, when all I wanted was to have a few drinks with friends. But then it turned into, "No more of this shit, I'm taking my lonely friend here to get his real birthday present!" and when the rest found out we were going to Tassels 'N' Tipples in North Beach—a place notorious for nefarious acts that often end in one going to the hospital for either a busted bone or a mysterious infection in the nether regions—they all decided to go their separate ways.

Wiping tears from my eyes and snot from my nose, I discover a black door in the black wall opposite the infinite row of black booths. I hear crying. I stand still. It takes me a while to realize it's not me who's crying and finally I open the door. It's a dark room filled with little vanity tables speckled in powders and spilt nail polishes, obviously the girls' dressing room. The whole space hangs heavy with a perfumed cloud that smells of cotton candy and sweat. At a table in the back of the room a woman sobs, her arms and head on the table. She's wearing a black silk robe. A few steps closer and I realize it's Syd.

"Syd? Syd, goddammit. I've been looking for you. Where'd you go? What the hell did you give me?" I ask, approaching her cautiously, though I don't know why, watching myself in her vanity mirror creeping closer and closer until my hand's on her heaving shoulder. She looks up and meets my eyes in the mirror. Her reading glasses are off and her black mascara has run. There's a small pile of photos on the table showing a little girl in a tire swing in front of a small suburban home, a yellow Mazda from the late 80s parked in the driveway. There's another of that little girl peeking over a crib at a baby surrounded by clown dolls. Another shows the family of four seated on the couch together, smiling, the father looking lovingly at the mother who stares directly into the camera lens trying not to collapse into a giggle-fit. The photo in Syd's left hand, however, is of herself as an adult standing before a large oval mirror, naked and hugging her own stretched, pregnant belly, a smile softening the corners of her lips. In that oval mirror you can see the photographer of the picture, but the flash and blur of the setting turned him into an apparition.

Her eyes like glassy marbles, Syd looks down at that picture then meets my eyes again in the mirror and says, "I only ever wanted a family, Luke. That's all I ever wanted," and more black tears trickle down her stained porcelain face. I notice that her fallen tears are dissolving the figures on the photos laid out before her, erasing the moments captured until all there is before her are squares of blank paper.

"Me, too, Syd," I tell her, meaning it with every fiber of my being. "My parents, though, they—"

A flash and blur explodes in the mirror over my right shoulder but when I turn around there's no one there, just the open door I came through swinging gently with a draft that gives me chills. When I turn back to Syd, she's no longer there, sitting at the vanity table. But she's still staring up at me with wet eyes from *within* the mirror, not moving, only staring and blinking and staring, her mouth slightly open as if frozen in the moment before saying something.

“Syd?” I ask and touch the mirror, but she doesn’t react, just continues to stare and blink. As cautiously as I approached her, I now back away from her reflection caught on loop in that mirror until I’m back in the eternal corridor of tainted stalls with their rustling curtains.

“Oh, for heaven’s sake, there you are,” a tall, thin man standing in front of a booth 20 feet away says. He’s wearing blue-green surgical scrubs, including gloves and the mask over his mouth. He’s holding the curtains to the booth open with one hand and waving me toward him with the other. “Come on now, dammit, we haven’t got all day now, do we? You were scheduled to go under eight minutes ago and we’re running so very very behind. This has to be done—this *all* has to be done in a timely, precise manner. We’re ready for you, we’re all ready for you—cleaned and scrubbed and prepped. Now get over here and quit wasting our time. You’re not our only patient, you know that don’t you?” he asks, straining to keep some sense of patience in his tone.

Standing next to him, he puts an arm around my shoulder and guides me into the booth, which is a bare operating room. There’s a sterile metal table in the middle of the room under a large lamp and there’s a modest team of surgeons and nurses standing there fidgeting with metal utensils or arranging tools on metal tables.

Despite it all there’s something very natural and comforting about this room, about this whole scene. I smile at the people who can't smile back because their faces are hidden and I glide to the metal table and slide onto it and stare up into the big burning lamp above me. I feel all warm and gooey again and it feels like love as the first scalpel incision carves into the left half of my torso. The surgeon works above me, cooing as if to a baby or kitten. Metal instruments come and go and get thrown into a clinking bucket out of view. It feels so good. It feels so right. I want to reach up and pet the surgeon or take one of the nurses by the hand and give it a good squeeze. Blood and pus and grey fluids leak out of me and it feels so relieving to have the pressure finally escape. Except, someone's screaming. Someone's screaming their fucking head off, wailing like a child that just got flipped over the handlebars of his little BMX and took a nosedive into the asphalt. Confused, and scared now, I look up at the surgeon who just keeps carving away at me. I reach for the nurses but they pull away from me. I put my hand on the surgeon's shoulder and he shrugs it off, more determined now at the carving, going faster and faster and faster. The screaming gets louder and louder and all my muscles tense up and this all seems so familiar again, but not natural, and not good. Then I realize the screaming is coming from near, very near, and it just keeps going, wailing and wailing at higher pitches. I can barely manage, but finally do turn my head down and to the left to where the surgeon is cutting and there's this mangled, bird-like creature there on the table, attached to my left side by ribbons of flesh but peeling away in a glistening redness of splitting meat and gristle.

Its eyes are wild and pleading and its three arms are flailing, gripping at my torso, trying to pull itself back to my side but unable to get a grip with all the blood covering us both.

It screams and screams and screams and I say, "Sammy, just let go. Just let go, little pigeon. Just let go, little brother." But he doesn't, even when the final swing of the scalpel removes him completely from my body. He just keeps swiping at me with all his tiny limbs, reaching for me until finally he slips and slides from the table like so much afterbirth, screaming for me, calling my name.

Though the surgeon tries to hold me back against the table, I jump from it and push everyone away and, naked and bleeding, back away from them toward the curtains, all of them with their hands out trying to calm me and convince me to return to the table because they need to finish the job. They're all blocking access to my clothes, which are behind them near the red-slickened metal table, but I spot my tidy whities at my feet and grab them, as well as a small towel that's folded up and stacked in a metal bowl. I step into my underwear, pulling them up, and push the towel hard against the gaping wound in my side, which makes the nearly forgotten puncture mark in my thigh look like nothing.

Then I'm falling through the curtains but I don't wind up back in the hallway. Instead, I'm in an Oregon highway rest area bathroom that I recognize for some reason, and I'm facing the mirror, and in the mirror is my 12-year-old self and I'm crying and there's a thunderous knocking at the door that rattles the doorframe and I don't want to open it but I'm compelled to. My uncle's large figure storms in and he asks if I'm having trouble again "tinkling" and I tell him I'm not and that I never have trouble and that I'm too old for the word "tinkling". But he's impatient and he pulls me over to the urinal by the waist of my jeans and tells me to hurry but I just stare at him and tell him I can't go with someone watching and he says "nonsense" while unbuckling my belt and unzipping my jeans and pulling my penis out and holding it, telling me to go, to just pee, goddammit, and he's holding onto it tight, and I push him away, screaming and bawling and sprint for the door.

And again I've not found my way back to the hallway. I'm now in the garage of my childhood home, the dirty afternoon sunlight sifting in through the smoked windows of the garage door. My heart's pounding and I'm still scared and bleeding and only in my underwear but I am overwhelmed with the need to hide so I slip under a tarp in the corner, unconcerned about the black widows I remember nesting there. It doesn't take long before I fall asleep. I wake to my parents standing over me and I'm small again, maybe five-years-old, and they're shaking their heads, mildly amused but mostly pissed off and they tell me I can't keep running off any time I feel like it and I tell them I was just playing with my friend, which sets a fire in my father's eyes and he yanks me by the arm to my feet and spanks me hard and tells me he doesn't want to hear another fucking thing about my imaginary friend and do I hear him and while crying and biting my little knuckles, trying to stifle my sobs and fear, I tell him I do. My mother picks me up and carries me out of the garage.

Which sends me tumbling into the wooded park on the outskirts of my childhood neighborhood and there's a shallow hole in the earth there near a large oak and there's a finger poking through at the bottom of the hole and I can't tell if it's human, animal, or stuffed animal, and before I can decide what to do I'm on all fours pushing mounds of dirt into the hole with hands and forearms until it's filled. Then I pat the earth flat and find some nearby fallen leaves and twigs and scatter them over it. I just sit there by the filled hole in the wooded park until dusk when suddenly beams of light swing in between the trees as people in badged uniforms and my neighbors and parents march through the woods calling for "little Lukey" and asking that I please come out and show myself. I can't, however, so I run out of the woods.

And into the hallway, which smells of old sex and baby powder.

Mmburr. Burrmmm. Mmburr. Burrmmm.

"For fuck's sake," I hear Syd from somewhere down the hall, which is no longer endless. "This fucking thing wouldn't work for me right earlier, either. I'm sorry, it'll just be a minute… but the wait will be worth it."

And the hallway becomes a cacophony of broken cash machines, porn, sticky flesh, and what sounds like someone shoving their whole arm into a barrel of spaghetti and stirring.

The lights flicker and I've got cotton mouth and I'm covered in vomit. I'm also cold. Very cold. And tired. Very tired. I just feel sick. I just feel so goddamned sick. And completely drained. I can't even remember what day it is or how I got here, or where here even is. Something at the backs of my eyes flashes and blurs and then something in my chest switches off and I close my eyes and sleep.

I come to in mid-stumble, being held up by someone much larger than me, and swaddled in a coat too big for me. My legs are bare and goosepimpled and it's all I can do to keep them from going out from under me. My feet are bare also and I realize all I have on are the strange coat and my Fruit of the Looms.

"Just take it easy now, Luke. Just take it easy, buddy. That's it," the voice to my left says and even though my balance is returning I lean into the source of that voice and find comfort in the large body there holding me up. We're walking through the lobby of Tassels 'N' Tipples toward the glass doors lit up with morning and leading out into the bustling day of North Beach.

The body to my left pulls away from me and opens the glass doors and gently guides me through them despite my feeble attempts to pull myself back to its side. I look back and it's Derrick who's helping me. He's now standing in the doorway, holding the door open, and I'm out under the strip club's marquee, cocooned in his jacket.

"I want to stay," I tell him.

"You can't, man. Come on now, you know that. You

can't stay forever. And I don't know that you should ever come back. You really think this is good for you? Christ, man, this can't keep happening. You expect me to drag your ass out of here week in, week out? You're a mess. You need help." His gaze is mixed with compassion and disgust.

"I want to stay!" I plead and he shakes his head and begins to retreat back inside but not before I block the door from shutting, thrusting his jacket at him, standing there desperate in my soiled underwear. "Derrick! Wait, wait, wait.... Your jacket! You need your jacket back, Derrick! It's a very nice jacket and you shouldn't lose it."

"Christ, Luke. What in hell are you talking about? Keep the damn thing. Like I'd even want it back with all that shit all over it now anyway, damn," he says, pushing my arm out of the doorway. Zombies stumble all about me under the marquee and giant crickets tickle my ears with their antennae while passing me.

Holding my filthy, naked self, Derrick's jacket gripped tightly in one hand, I plead once more in a near-whisper, "But, Derrick, I don't want to go. Please… don't make me go."

"Would you quit with that *Derrick* shit, man? You've been coming here for an eternity. You know damn well my name's Sam, Luke." Then he shakes his head again and says "shit" and pulls inside the club, locking that and the other glass doors before strolling away from them back into the darkness.

With the sun excruciatingly close and rising slow and huge above me, I turn and, with the jacket stretched out behind me like a cape, smile wide and run like a superhero about to take flight, chasing down every pigeon I see, kicking at them and stomping them flat in the gutters, and laughing, laughing, laughing through rotting teeth. When not chasing pigeons or avoiding the lepers, I try to find my way back home, biting my nails to the quick and watching my bare feet the whole way to make sure I don't step on anything sharp.

BLUE MONSTER

As she unfurls her slender, naked form and stands up from the bed, tired and slick with new sweat, the glow of the late night street lamp outside the window sets her right arm aflame. She's burning, the flame licking up and down her arm like a blue and orange lizard's tongue, though she doesn't flinch or scream out, so I don't worry.

"What the *fuck* is that?" I ask as the flame fizzles and goes out. A white fog pulls away from her body with a whispering whistle and dissipates. She bends over for a second as if punched in the gut, her hands on the bed, then looks up and smiles, embarrassed. I reach out to her from the bed, then think better of it and pull back and touch myself, instead, and stroke my dick while looking at her beautiful body to try and calm myself and bring myself back to reality. It doesn't work.

"What?" she asks, pulling away from the bed and

standing up, two handfuls of breasts and a hollow belly gone white.

I grab her right arm and point to where the flame had been, "That! What the fuck is *that*?"

"I don't know what you're talking about, Luke," she says, laughing in one short gasp that turns into a small grunt as I yank her arm, pull her back onto the bed and point at it.

"That. That, right fucking there. What the hell is that?" I ask with eyes wide, ignoring the beastly yelps and grunts eschewing from the filthy Tenderloin street below. I ignore the sounds of thrusting, the wet and dull sounds of meat slamming into meat, the jagged, Velcro-like tearing sounds of limbs ripped off and the screams of ecstasy it causes. The sounds of body parts dropping against asphalt. The sounds of rain that come after each thud to wash it all into the storm drains that are stopped up and full of thick black and red swirling puddles, twigs, used condoms, and wedding rings still on dismembered fingers.

"My tattoo? Jesus, Luke. My fucking tattoo? Is that what you're going on about? Jesus. It's just my blue bulldog. What's gotten into you?" Her voice goes soft and scared. The light coming through the curtains continues to blow the room around in a dirty orange hue.

"That's not a fucking bulldog. That's a fucking monster, Cameron. That's a monster," I say, jabbing my finger at the blue monster, but not touching it.

"Um, okay, Luke," she says, unnerved.

She tries to spill from the bed again, but I catch her arm once more and pull her back. An eruption of giggles. She falls into me and tries to stroke me with her right hand but I don't want that thing anywhere near me so I push her arm away and give her a look that implies I'm in a serious mood.

"Cameron, it's on the wrong fucking arm! Your fucking tattoo has always—*always*—been on your left arm, Cameron. What the fuck are you trying to pull?"

"You are losing it. You really are," she says, grabbing her smokes from the nightstand and lighting a menthol cigarette. As she moves the cigarette back and forth from her lips, ribbons of mint-green smoke snake toward the browning ceiling. While she watches smoke rise, I watch that blue, sinewy monster crawl from her right arm across her body and slide like oil onto her pale stomach and position itself there on all fours, blood leaking from its teeth.

"There! There! You see?" I say, pointing at her stomach where the blue monster lies motionless.

"I'm losing patience. See what? See what now, Luke?" she asks, arms out, mocking me by looking all over herself and the room.

"It's on your goddamned stomach now. Yesterday, and every day before that, that blue monster was on your left arm. Then, suddenly it's on your right? Now it's on your stomach! What the fuck are you doing, Cameron? What are you trying to pull, goddammit?"

She guffaws, slips from the bed, puts the menthol out, and laughs again while standing bedside and petting her belly in slow, circular strokes.

"My little blue bulldog has always been on my stomach, Luke," she says in a baby voice, pretend-petting the blue thing on her belly. "I think you'd have been fully aware of that by now as it's not too far away from the part about me you like best," she says in an annoyed grown-up voice, giving me a look.

"No. No, Cameron. That's not true. You're trying to do something here, but I don't know what. I don't understand. Help me understand," I say in a pleading voice, leaning on my side and looking up at her with eyes that must be tearing up by now.

"You just need a drink," she says with an exaggerated nod, mocking me still.

Returning from the adjacent kitchen, she hands me a glass of whiskey. "Take your medicine, big boy," she says.

Outside, sirens scream out. Inside, red, blue, and white lights circle the room and block out the orange light of the street lamp. Outside, police bust windows of storefronts and tell everyone to get back while they wait for backup. The Orkin people soon arrive and the sound of a thousand crickets dying screeches throughout 10 city blocks. After people clap their ears closed to muffle the terrible noise they clap and cheer and congratulate each other while the room Cameron and I are in clouds up with poison. Then everything quiets again and it's just the dirty orange light of the street lamp filling the room through a window with billowing curtains. The only sound in the room is wind and breath.

I sit up in bed, back against the wall. Animal noises creep in from the street below again. There's the scuffle of zombies crawling on hands and knees begging for a nickel while giving head to off-duty bartenders that sell drugs to supplement their meager incomes and have tentacles instead of arms and third eyes that leak a thick, syrupy black ink. That black eye-syrup is sold by gypsies from street carts around San Francisco as aphrodisiacs that increase sperm count so the world can fill itself with more zombies.

I take a sip of the whiskey. My stomach howls and unleashes belts of bile that whip up my esophagus to coat the roof of my mouth. I take another sip and wash it down. I take another sip to bring it all back. And repeat.

"I have to take a piss," Cameron says, holding her hands up, palms out. "Calm yourself."

I make eye contact with her as she stands there, tell her I love her and that I just want her to come back to bed—that I'm sorry for becoming irrational, insane, unreasonable, and confused. I say I must be mistaken, that if she says the tattoo of a blue bulldog—not a monster—has always been on her beautifully pale belly, then I believe her. That even if I've lapped at her belly button and wrapped my lips around her clit and sucked, that even though I did those things with eyes open many a night to witness her stomach muscles contract and release with each lubricated sound, that I must, despite those memories, be mistaken about the placement of her blue beast.

Then I notice the blue monster slither down her stomach, crawl over her pussy, and stop on her inner thigh, its sides heaving from the effort. The blood from its mouth drips down her leg, leaves a small puddle where she stands before she turns down the hallway for the bathroom.

In bed, I pull myself up straighter against the wall, take large gulps of the whiskey, light up a Winston Light, and try to relax. Two of my front teeth turn to ice, fall into the glass to keep it cold.

I drink it all down and nearly choke.

"Feeling better now?" she asks upon her return, crawling into bed and curling up against me as if she might purr.

"What the *fuck*?" I say, jumping from beneath her and out of bed. Leaning over, I push her onto her back and inspect her naked figure from top to bottom. She giggles. I flip her on her stomach.

"Oh, are we going *there* now?" she asks, laughing excitedly.

I roll her onto her back once more in the orange glow.

"Where'd it go, Cameron?" I ask, almost furious now, but too frightened to be truly mad.

"Where'd what go, Luke?" she asks through half-moon eyelids, suddenly sleepy.

"Your tattoo. Your tattoo, for fuck's sake!"

"I don't know what you're talking about, for fuck's sake," she says, mocking me.

"Don't do this. It was there. It was right there!" I say, pointing a finger hard into her inner thigh.

"Ouch! Enough of the rough stuff. Fix me a drink if you want to play that way," she says, slurring her speech, rolling over, and arching her back slightly so her ass sticks up in the air.

I put my Winston out in the ashtray on the nightstand. Grunts and snuffs come from the street below. I roll her onto her back and look her all over again. She laughs. There's blood. There's a blood trail. I see it coming in from the hallway. It follows her up onto the bed. It's growing beneath her, soaking her sheets in darkness.

"You had a tattoo. You did," I say, almost sobbing, defeated. "You had a tattoo of a blue monster. It's been on your left arm for as long as I've known you. Then it was just on your right. Then your stomach. Then on the inside of your thigh. Now, it's gone. It's fucking gone, Cameron. Where did it go? Where the fuck could it have gone?" I ask, feeling sleepy, now, myself.

"You're crazy. You're just crazy, Luke. You always have been crazy. Come into bed. Come," she says, her arms out and open to me.

"But… but you're bleeding. Cameron, goddammit, you're bleeding," I say, suddenly exhausted from it all.

"No," she says. "No. No, I'm not silly. Don't be silly.

Don't be a dummy." She keeps her arms held out for me.

Orange light pools in my eyeballs and everything I see is filtered through a hazy orange film. It's as if I'm suddenly wearing 50-pound weights around my head and neck and eyelids. Dragged down, I crawl into bed and into her arms and fall asleep immediately.

When I wake it's still a filthy orange light that fills the room. The air is warm, now, though. And it's quiet. The clock says it's tomorrow. I'm covered in sheets of blood. She is, too. But she's breathing. Soundly. Her narrow spine moves with each breath.

I go to the kitchen, clank some ice into my glass and drown it in whiskey, a few drops of the blood coating my skin plop into the golden liquid and give it a faint orange hue. Then I return to the room where Cameron sleeps, slick with blood in an orange room. All orange. The bed. The walls. The curtains. The nightstands. All painted a bright orange and dimly lit. And her red body in the middle of it.

I sit back on the orange bed with my orange whiskey and blow blue smoke for hours until she wakes.

"Morning, sunshine," she says, rubbing her eyes with blood-caked hands to remove the blood that's glued her eyelids shut. Eight a.m. light fills the room and dapples our sticky red bodies. Only then do I notice the room is no longer orange. It's blue. Blue from floorboards to walls and ceiling. The curtains are blue. The light's blue. The same shade of Cameron's non-existent tattoo.

I don't say anything. Light another Winston. Sip the remnants of long-melted ice and warm whiskey. Outside, everything has died and gone quiet. Everything that once had life, anyway. There's still the sounds of people going to work and buses running them over, of course.

"I'm sorry," I say.

"Oh, Luke. You don't have to apologize. I know how you get sometimes. You're what I call *quirky*—it's what I like about you. You're unpredictable. You have nothing to apologize for," she says to me with sweet sincerity, completely caked in blood.

"No, I'm really sorry," I say, still refusing to look at her.

"And, really, it's not a big deal," she says, pulling herself up in bed to sit against the blue wall beside me, our red bodies shoulder to shoulder.

"I'm so sorry, Cameron."

"What are you sorry for, huh? What?" she asks and puts a hand on my upper thigh, all red and tacky. It's a touch that would normally send powerful gushes of blood flooding into my cock, stiffening it and readying it for her red mouth or pussy, but nothing's moving down there now. I feel like nothing ever will again.

I take a drag from my Winston, look toward the window, and I can't feel the smoke enter or exit my lungs. I can't even tell if I'm breathing. I can't hear my breath or the wind.

"Luke. What are you sorry for?" she asks, real concern creeping into her voice.

"I'm sorry Toby died."

"Luke, that's just sick. That's just—"

"I'm sorry he died. I know he was just a kid."

"Please, don't make sick jokes about my goddamned son," she says sternly, removing her sticky hand from my sticky leg.

"I don't understand it. I don't know how it happened. I'm sorry, Cameron. I'm sorry he died that way. I'm so sorry. I am. I really am." I still can't look at her. I still can't feel the smoke.

"If you're going to continue saying fucked up shit, Luke, just—just get the hell out."

"I'm sorry. There was nothing I could do," I say. I smoke. I almost cry. But I don't. I just don't feel like it.

She gets out of bed, wraps herself in a robe and gives me a look before heading out into the hallway, leaving red bloody footprints in her wake all over the blue floors.

When she gets to Toby's room down the hall she screams. She screams for hours. I imagine she also cries. I imagine she tears at her eyes and hair and pounds her chest and rips her own flesh. But I only know for sure that she screams.

I stay in that bed until the light changes back to burnt orange and the room changes back to orange and the blood dries and turns to dust and disintegrates. I stay there smoking until the pack empties while the room goes from orange to blue, back to orange again. Cameron never returns. I can't decide if I miss her or not. I can't decide what to do next. The room spins and keeps changing between the two colors. Time becomes a colored liquid. I stay in that bed for weeks—unaware of whose bed it actually is—with a scream crashing over and over again against the inside of my increasingly brittle skull. Then the room goes black.

GETTING THERE

I wake to an animal tearing out of my chest, and I grunt and push myself up and back on my elbows, kicking the sheets and covers off the bed as I attempt to focus my sleepy, blurry vision on the dark thing that scurries out of me and into the corner of the room, out of sight.

Lunging out of bed I step on a beer can, yell out, and kick the can aside, then carefully walk over to the corner where I thought I'd seen the thing run. I push the fake ficus in a wicker basket aside. There's nothing there but lint, dust, hair.

Confused. And not sure if I had been dreaming. But this happens all the time. So, I try to breathe past the bruise in my chest.

My Xanax sits atop the TV that I never turn off and now shows news of a bridge collapse in the Midwest. Distracted, I hear the news anchor say, "…diverted money from bridge maintenance to…." I pop a couple pills and swallow them dry. "Yes, that's right, Hannah. Possibly 30 or more trapped in the 40-degree water under the rubble."

It's 8:30 a.m. It's my 30th birthday.

At the window, three stories up, I stand in just my boxers and watch traffic roll down Leavenworth and Post streets. My apartment building is located at the bottom of Nob Hill and above a café filled with red velvet couches, red velvet curtains, and lots of open space. It's what's known as a "soft foundation" for a building and I know I'm destined to die in a quake when the earth shakes and sends a cartoon-like snowball of people, cars, and buildings from the top of the hill down to slam right into my solitary confinement. I expect to live for up to 17 hours underneath it all, however, suffering through whistling breaths of crushed lungs and the pain of a pulverized pelvis and dismembered left leg. Two days after my neighbors and I are dug out and later buried, cars will traffic the street again, and while not everyone forgets, everyone gets by and, as they pass the intersection of my painful death, they'll briefly recall the rubble and bodies that recently laid here but quickly push it all aside as it makes their morning coffees taste like gas fumes and it's all just too much to think about.

Now, I move my gaze from my future death and a perfectly busy downtown intersection and look up to see the old woman that lives across the way watching me through coyly parted curtains. She's in a white robe, her hair wrapped in a white towel, looking like a mummy coming unwrapped.

Making eye contact with the nosy old bat, I slowly slip my hand down my chest and my stomach, lift the elastic band of my boxers, and reach in and grab my cock and start tugging. Her eyes widen and I blow her a kiss and really give my morning wood a meaningful yank for the wrinkly wench, hoping to shock her enough to leave the window or die from a fucking heart attack. Only thing is, she's also giving herself a good wank so I put a halt to all proceedings, pivot away from the window, whistle casually and put a pot on the small, electric two-burner to boil water for my morning coffee.

When I turn back around a few minutes later and look out the window I see nothing, fortunately, but a Peregrine falcon perched on the fire escape of the old penis-woman's building. There's a pigeon trapped in the falcon's talons. Every few seconds, with a mechanical, jerky plunge, it snaps its sharp beak into the pigeon, ripping feathers out one by one, dropping a tickertape parade of lice- and flea-infested feathers to the sidewalk below. There's nothing I can do but watch.

My cell rings. The screen says "Mom" and I let it ring. The bridge on the TV is not getting any better and it looks like no one knows what to do with the situation. Just a bunch of helicopters flying around and some lights flashing, but, really, nothing much is happening besides people drowning in the river, unconscious within their busted up cars.

That bridges can collapse, just like that, fills me with way too much anxiety and I try to remember that I already took some Xanax but can't keep myself from going back to the TV and popping another one. And then another. "We're hearing there was a school bus on the bridge when it collapsed… can you confirm that for us, Jim?" the news anchor asks. And maybe just a half-one more, which I bite off and chew.

In the bathroom, I fish some Advil out of the medicine cabinet and pop four of those. In the mirror of the medicine cabinet I see there's a red mark on my chest and some scrapes, scratches, and discoloring, and I wonder what the fuck I could have been doing to myself in my sleep.

I've hurt myself plenty in my sleep before. I've woken up slamming my head into walls, walking into doors, and I've been told by girlfriends that didn't stick around too long that I often would pummel myself in my sleep with both fists while weeping profusely and calling for my brother. It especially confused and scared them because I don't have a brother. But this looks like I was clawing at my chest as if I was trying to tear out my own heart. Perhaps if I'd done that while sleeping next to my past girlfriends they would have found me romantic and stuck around.

The cell rings again. The screen says "Lowry" and I pick up. "Happy Birthday! You ready to see the ponies?" Lowry asks.

For a second I'm confused. "Pennies?"

"Horses, man. The horsies!"

"Lowry, the bridge collapsed."

"Huh? The bridge? What bridge? The Bay Bridge?"

"Yeah."

"What the fuck are you talking about, man? No bridge collapsed."

"If you try to get from here to there, you need a bridge. And it collapsed like it was never there in the first place. And it killed people—children, even. But not immediately. They all had to suffocate first by filling their lungs full of river water. It hurt. A lot. I was there. I was there with them. It fucking hurt, Lowry."

"I don't know what you're on this morning, Luke, my man, but you'll have to share some when we meet up."

"Oh, yeah. Yeah, um, just… give me a minute. I just woke up. I feel like shit."

"What's new, Luke?" Lowry says and guffaws.

I guffaw back and hang up.

Thirty minutes later I'm in a cab with Lowry heading toward the CalTrain station where I'm told there's a bar so we can grab a couple bloody marys and meet everyone else before heading out to Bay Meadows Racetrack in San Mateo.

Lowry goes on and on about his dreads, his ex-girlfriend, his near-romantic love of some Giants pitcher, how his skateboard has new wheels that roll "like hell," and how he's got so many women in his back pocket now that he's a free man that it'd make Chamberlain look like a chump.

I smile, then feel sick to my stomach as I try to forget the black rat in the shower this morning that crawled up my leg and sank its fangs into my inner thigh before I could swat it away—I try to forget how I fell over in the bath tub, grazing my head against the water spout as the shower curtain broke away from the rod with the weight of the rat's body and crashed down to the floor. Then, how that wet thing wrestled its way out from the translucent shower curtain and ran out of the bathroom and down the short hallway into the main room. There was nowhere for it to hide but I didn't find anything in my little studio.

The inner part of my left thigh, now, is bright red, but not bleeding. I rub it for a bit until I notice Lowry giving me a weird look, so I stop.

After an unbearable amount of time wondering how I choose my friends we finally end up at the CalTrain station only to find out that the bar doesn't open up until the afternoon. So, Lowry and I walk up toward the Giants ballpark to find a new bar and my sister calls and I don't answer and then my voicemail alert beeps and I listen to my sister singing me "Happy Birthday" and then I put the phone away and tell Lowry that if we don't find a bar fast I will lose my mind and he says not to worry and before I know it we're sitting in an elaborate Irish pub with gorgeous dark wood fixtures and beams and Lowry buys my first bloody mary and says "Happy 30th," and, feeling a tidal wave of anguish and gratitude, I have to hold back from crying. Then I say thanks, clink glasses, and enjoy this bloody mary at 9:30 in the morning.

After a few more drinks and Jim Beam shots I'm feeling in control, so Lowry and me head to the train station where we greet my friends who look less than enthused, obviously tired, hungover, drugged out, and mostly bored.

We take some celebratory group photos where I pretend I'm dead and my friends grieve over me. Other pictures are full of ass-slapping (not my idea) and lewd gestures—lots of middle fingers and tongues sticking out and one, I think, of a baseball bat being swung hard against my head, my brain jutting out in chopped up bits through my mouth, my eyeballs bulging and my hands out in an "It's a Party" dancing gesture.

On the train, my head throbs. It's rolling too slow, or too fast or just not the right way and turns my stomach. Kevin looks at me with his curly hair and gangliness and laughs and says, "Luke, come on, buddy. It ain't the end of the world," and he throws me an MGD from his backpack. And because Kevin makes everyone feel better just because, I feel better for a second. I crack open the MGD and take a sip and try to keep feeling better.

When I look out the window of the train now going way too fast I see a nuclear bomb exploded in the distance, but then think it's probably just steam from a factory. Then I get a call from Wilson, who is usually pretty good at coming through in the end, despite his inability to answer a single question clearly or make definite plans; however, I don't pick up, don't hear a voicemail beep, and eventually get a text that he's not making it out to the track with us—that he'll buy me a drink later after the horses have finished circling my 30-year gallop toward death.

Lowry and Kevin are talking and I look at Sanchez who

hasn't said much since meeting up and he looks at me, looks around the train, takes a brief glance out the window, then back at me, sticks one finger into his mouth and mimics vomiting.

I look back out the train window to a quickly pulled zipper of nuclear explosions opening up the land.

Russ—a rather large guy with a rather small lesbian girlfriend—is complaining about being up all night fucking.

"She's just insatiable, man," he says, looking down, rubbing his forehead perplexedly, sighing and seeming altogether worn out. "But her pussy is just too good! I can't say no."

Lowry leans across the aisle, gives him a high-five and I try to imagine Russ and his girlfriend having sex and I can only imagine that Russ is the only one actually getting fucked in that scenario.

The scenery outside the train window is of rolling hills, green pastures, blue lagoons, some views of the Pacific, trees, and absolutely no life. Nothing, outside of the earth, is moving out there.

Big puffs of white mushroom in the distance.

Russ and Kevin sit across the aisle from me, Lowry and Sanchez sit in chairs directly across from me.

"What's going on, asshole?" I ask Sanchez, kicking him in the shin.

"Don't fucking kick me, asshole, okay?" Sanchez says.

"Hey, fuckwad, it's my birthday, you know? I can do whatever I want." Then I kick him in the other shin, hard, and he almost gets up out of his chair like he's going to kick my ass, but thinks better of it.

Something dark scuttles down the aisle past my foot. Sanchez goes on about his ex-wife, which I find hilarious, since they were married all of seven months, and that marriage happened in a drunken brainstorming about eight fucking months ago that lead them to Vegas. Her name was Jasmine but she looked like Cleopatra. He goes on about the abortion and how he talked her into it, how he should have had the kid with her, not pushed her into the decision, which caused the breakup and her to move to L.A. He says he's worried she's become a junky and doesn't know what to do. He says he wants to be a family man.

"She felt the need to leave San Francisco to become a junky? Are you fucking kidding me?" I ask, thinking of how many needles I have to pull out of my arms before getting on the bus in the morning.

His eyes water. White light fills the train car before it starts to pull apart at the seams and disintegrate in scalding ripples.

"Seriously?" I ask, trying to sound more sincere and interested and as if I could actually care. Sanchez doesn't answer, just sighs and averts his eyes. More often than he should, he smoothes his pencil 'stache with thumb and forefinger.

I look over to Russ and Kevin yukking it up, having a grand old time as bright lights flash over and over again through the windows behind them.

“Hey, Russ, you’re kind of fat. Why don’t you stop eating for a week or so? A month, even,” I say.

Russ stops in the middle of telling a humorous story and looks over to me, halts his own chuckle, and says, “What, Luke?”

“You’re fat, dude. You make me sick,” I say, nearly spitting.

Russ, a sad, confused look on his face, looks over himself and asks again, “What?”

“Nothing,” I say. I look at Kevin, reach over the aisle into his backpack and grab myself another MGD then walk back toward the bathroom. I hear a bunch of “what’s his problem” kind of stuff behind me.

My phone rings again, vibrates in my pocket. It’s Aunt Annie. I haven’t heard from Annie in ages and I, now, actually, can’t remember if she’s my mom’s sister or my dad’s or if she’s just some lady that lived down the street. I do remember her sneaking me sips from her glasses of Tullamore Dew when I was six and always feeling warm from that. I also liked that it was one of many secrets we kept from my mom and dad.

Distracted, the train car fills with white light when I realize Aunt Annie is telling me about San Diego and how she’s been sky diving and playing billiards at the neighborhood pub and meeting plenty of nice older gentleman.

“I’ve got rats,” I say.

“What’s that, sweetheart?”

"Rats. They're everywhere. I think one bit my thigh earlier in the shower. A bridge collapsed. I'm not really sure about the structural soundness of my building. But I've definitely got rats."

"I met the nicest man just the other night—"

"And my chest hurts."

"…and he knew all about—"

"I'm not sure if they're actually there. It's my birthday, by the way."

"…different kinds of vaginal problems, because he's a gynecologist, it turns out—"

"I've got rats," I say and hang up.

I think about how much I can't remember. I think about how much I choose to remember. I think about how it's my birthday and I can do whatever I want.

Suddenly, I recall that I was on this same train when a woman jumped in front of it. Before I can feel sick about that I'm overwhelmed with understanding, empathy, and an unfamiliar sense of longing, love, and lust. I want to *feel* that woman's warmth against me before and after the train ripped her to shreds.

Then, in the tiny bathroom of the CalTrain, I down a can of MGD while pissing and choking myself to keep from crying as I recall the terrified and sad look on the engineer's face when he came running toward the back of the train after hitting the woman. It took a long time before we rolled on to the next stop because her body was in the way of our train. People were confused and upset and tired and bored while a body with its chest torn open was being peeled from the tracks, its bones sticking to them, her brain all over the stones and entangled in the grill of the train.

I pop another Xanax while at the toilet when a sharp pain in the back of my neck ignites. I drop the pill bottle into the toilet, let out a yelp, pivot around and see this huge, wet, diseased black rat with back arched, one foot much larger than the other, hissing in the corner of the small room. I jump up on the toilet but there's no lid so one foot lands in the toilet and the other on the rim and I scream, again, embarrassing myself as it happens, and the rat keeps hissing, and then it's up on its hind legs and lunging for me and I shield my face, turn away, slip hard off the metal toilet. I hit my lower back against it and fall to the floor, slamming against the close walls of the restroom with a hollow thud as I do. Then, sitting there on the floor, dazed, with one elbow up on the rim of the toilet, I crumple up, repress the urge to vomit, and cry a little into my hands.

Somehow the rat must have squeezed under the door or jumped into the toilet and wiggled its way down into the train's septic tank, because it's not here now.

Back at my seat across from Sanchez and Lowry, I massage the back of my neck and just try to get comfortable and remain calm. Neither of them notice my right pants leg is soaked and smells like piss.

Sanchez and Lowry are having a conversation about baseball statistics, pussy, and how they plan to make money at the horse track today. Russ and Kevin are playing a game of Rock, Paper, Scissors, and complaining about the long 45-minute trip.

"Lowry," I say.

"Yeah?"

"You got a cigarette?"

"You're smoking one, Luke."

I notice that I am. "I mean, another one. I'm out after this."

He adjusts his dreads, gives me a quizzical look.

"It's my birthday," I say.

"I know. Yeah, here you go." He hands me a Kool and I try not to grimace or give him a dirty look.

"Smoke with me," I say and motion to the back of the train.

Tasting mentholly shittiness hit the back of my throat, I say, "I don't know what's going on."

"What are you talking about?"

"Is the world ending?"

He pa-shaws me, takes a drag and looks around.

I stare at him. Lights flash behind my eyes. Black rats pour in from the other train car.

"Jesus, Luke, turning 30 is not the end of the world."

I pull my shirt down from the neck and show him the marks on my chest. He grimaces and steps back.

"What do you think that's from?" I ask.

He looks at me. Takes another drag.

"Do you think I did this to myself?"

He feigns a smile, pats me on the shoulder and walks back to his seat.

"Wait…" I say, too quietly, then head back to my seat, leaving the menthol behind to burn out on the train's carpeted aisle.

The inner part of my thigh flames up. The back of my neck pulses. My lower back throbs. But not as much as my chest aches, and while the light keeps flashing, even though it's daytime, I keep wondering what time it is. I keep thinking about the lady this train, this very train hit, and how she might have talked. I imagine an accent, but one you can't quite put a finger on. I imagine a flowing sundress and long, sun-bleached hair. I imagine a mouth like a crescent moon showing in an autumn day. I imagine pressing my lips to that mouth before she would ever have thought of jumping in front of a train. Then I imagine pushing my lips against hers after she had, trying hard to breathe life back into them and instead how I would pull her lips free from her face and how they would stick to mine for at least a week until finally chapping and falling off in black flakes.

I get sick and vomit onto the feet of Sanchez and Lowry and they both pretend not to notice.

It's my birthday. It's my 30th. And the train comes to a squealing halt.

The engineer suddenly runs toward the back of the car and I feel nothing behind my ribcage but an emptiness that hurts somehow, like an empty tin can being kicked around, just a dull ache, a sensation I don't like. For an instant, I wonder if the bridge we're on has collapsed, but remember we're not on a bridge. As always, I'm firmly rooted to the ground.

Then my leg falls asleep and my neck feels like it might snap off if I take another look at explosions and mushroom clouds.

"Hey, Luke," Kevin says, holding me by the back of the neck. "Snap out of it, man. Shit, what's your problem? It's just a minor delay. Here, have another beer. Jesus, try enjoying your birthday a little bit, man. Chill out!"

He hands me another beer and I smile, pretend like nothing is happening, that the world outside isn't blowing up and that something out there or inside me isn't trying to destroy me, or that we didn't just hit another person, that every train I'm on is not destined to kill somebody.

A scorching bright light blossoms out the window and I flinch.

Then nothing happens.

I'm a little disappointed. I open the beer and down half of it as quickly as possible and Sanchez and Lowry give me high-fives, telling me I know the exact right way to start off a new decade of my life.

Yes, the future's so bright, I gotta wear shades.

The woman's body lies outside, having been cut to shreds by the train's iron wheels. Unfortunately, her head and a portion of her bisected torso are about 30 yards in front of the train, while the other part of her torso is about 30 yards behind the train. One of her legs flew up the bordering embankment, where it's found, but the other has disappeared. The investigating team wonders if she even had a second leg or if she hobbled here, via crutch and will, to take the train's full force—whether she worked even harder than most to meet the hard kiss of the train's grill.

On the stalled train, no one else seems to be taking notice of this tragedy, this sadness, this sickness that I'm witnessing. No one else seems to have a moment's thought toward this. Even when outside the window I see a man in a Hazmat suit place her head in a clear plastic bag and seal it. He hands it to another man in a Hazmat suit that writes something on the bag that I can't quite read. I'm just saddened seeing that her hair is red, knowing it's not her natural color.

Between conversations revolving around on-base percentage and strikeouts-to-walks ratios as well as the quality of women who shave their pussies versus those that don't and the tragedy it is that no guy could ever actually tell a woman she has a big pussy and how the latest episode of *Lost* was complete bullshit, the train finally lurches forward with no explanation and no sign of the engineer having gone back to the train's controls.

My cell rings and the screen reads "Dad" and I let it ring

until I hear the voicemail alert beep. Then I listen to my dad sing "Happy Birthday" while the train seems to be riding over a warped and bumpy track, the sky outside turning quickly to violent lightning storms then back to partly-clouded skies.

Sanchez and Lowry keep chatting, downing their beers while laughing. Russ and Kevin are busting a gut across the aisle from me, their innards spilling out into the aisle between us. Rats lick at their intestines and call in their friends.

Like I said, Kevin makes everyone laugh.

"Hey, Kevin," I say, reaching across the aisle, smacking his forearm before grabbing another beer from his backpack and getting nipped by one of the rats.

Russ and Kevin stop laughing. A large rat runs up the backs of their seats and disappears. I take a long pull on the beer and then ask for a cigarette, which Kevin passes onto me and I light it and drink the beer and keep looking at Russ and Kevin and wait for the rat to come back. Then I see it, under their seats, waiting, scared and sickly but ready to bite me again, to take another piece of me with it. But I know now, more than anything, it's just scared. Like me.

"Hey! Kevin!" I yell again, then feel something nibble at my ankles. Lights outside flash and flicker. I smell burning flesh. It smells like tomato soup and beans.

"Shit, Luke, I'm listening! What? What is it?" Kevin says, smiling.

I take a drag from my cigarette and gesture toward

Lowry who's laughing away about something juvenile with Sanchez. "You know I fucked his girlfriend, right?" I say.

Russ leans over Kevin, tries to play the diplomat, "Look, Luke, you're drunk. Come on, man. Just be cool."

"Fuck you, Russ," I say, spewing smoke out of all the holes that have formed in my body over the last few years. Then I take another drag from the cigarette and another pull on the can of beer. "You don't even care that we just ran over someone, do you?" I plead. "That we, us, all of us, just ripped someone to shreds. You don't even care that they put this poor woman's head in a bag. All anyone can think about is the delay! How long it will take! When they will get there! Who gives a fuck! No one is going *anywhere*, anyway! Fuck!"

"What?" Russ asks. "Um, Luke, what are you talking about?"

I lean over the aisle again and say, "Fuck you, Russ. Fuck you. That's what I'm talking about. Go get fucked by your lesbian girlfriend."

"Jesus, Luke, what's gotten into you?" Kevin asks.

Finally Lowry says, "Luke, did you say you fucked my girlfriend?"

"Ex-girlfriend," I say, blowing more smoke.

"Whatever! Did you fuck Sherry? Is that who you're talking about? And when? Luke, when the fuck did this even happen, man?" he asks, now standing in front of me.

"You're an idiot, Lowry. You'll never make it in the

Bigs," I say and toss my empty beer can at him. Almost simultaneously and with superhuman speed I grab another beer from Kevin's backpack, trying not to get bitten again by the river of frightened rats. You can see it in all their eyes—we make *them* nervous, not the other way around.

There's protest all around me. The rats pile up at me feet, nibble at my toes, wrestle at my ankles, shins, and knees.

I thought my chest ached, but it doesn't. Not anymore.

"Nobody cares that we just killed somebody because we just *had* to get somewhere! But we're not going anywhere, and never were! We just keep rolling over body after body getting there, and…" I yell, feeling a sudden loss of energy and meaning.

"Christ, Luke, you're crazy! Shut the fuck up and calm down," Kevin demands from across the aisle. Lowry still stands over me, threateningly.

"Why would you say that?" Lowry asks.

"Because we did. We killed her. Just going nowhere, on our way to nothing. We killed her."

"Luke!" Lowry says, his dreads shimmering in the violently flashing lights pulsing in through the windows.

The rats pile up and bite my stomach, try to burrow into my crotch. I grimace but do my best not to let on.

"Listen, Lowry, I fucked your girlfriend. Russ is a fat, pathetic suck-up. Sanchez is a closet homo that can't face it, and Kevin, well, Kevin just tries too damned hard."

The train comes to a sudden, abrupt halt again, and all

my guts go flying out of my mouth toward the front of the train car in one flow of red and purple ribbon.

Then, just daylight through the train's windows. Pleasant autumn daylight. Soft. Inviting. Comforting. No rats. No bombs. No bodies vivisected. No one. No one at all.

The conductor calls out the destination of Bay Meadows. I leave my friends behind, glued to their seats, and step off the train, put on my Wayfarers, and feel a slight pain in my leg, back, chest, and neck. I stretch, do some neck rolls, get some blood flowing, then light a cigarette and walk toward the horse track with a limp and $60 in my pocket. When I get to the track, all the horses' heads have fallen off and there's no one around except the dozens of jockeys weeping into the dirt and pounding their chests, inconsolable and covered in horse blood under a low, overcast sky.

OLD MAN BILL
or
DOG!

It's just me and Old Man Bill. He's sitting next to me at Bourbon Bandits in his floppy hat and khaki windbreaker mumbling, fingering his ear, inspecting the wax left on his fingertips, and popping his dentures in and out of place. It makes a wet suction sound and a hard clack each time. Each time he laughs and looks around, googly-eyed beneath the hat's brim, to see if anyone enjoyed his little joke, then he goes back to fingering his ear and mumbling and watching the TV in the corner that plays a boxing match that sometimes turns into a camcorder video of my mother's splitting vagina spewing blood in order to let my head and shoulders exit into this world. The doctor, nurses, and my father keep trying to push me back in, but I'm a rotten, determined bastard and manage to slip out and fall to the floor with the rest of the mucus and stringy grey filaments filling my mother. Then it's just two men dancing in a ring and punching each other again.

Overhead, Clap Your Hands Say Yeah's "In This Home On Ice" is playing because I put it on the Internet jukebox because I just came from their show around the corner at Great American and I'm already feeling sentimental about the time I spent there dancing and throwing up into the nearby trashcan at the back of the dance floor and telling Kevin how much fun I was having anyway and how he would smirk and look away, embarrassed, and I would pretend not to notice and his girlfriend would lean into him as though she was scared of something. Then I would wipe the vomit from my grin and keep dancing and eye the bartender in the corner and feel even better because she had blonde hair and no monster tattooed on her arm and her breasts would glisten under the strobe lights and seem welcoming.

Just now the ghost of Abigail walks in through the black rectangle of the open doorway into this black rectangle of a bar called Bourbon Bandits. Even though I know I left her bleeding out months ago in the green backstage rooms of the Great American, I also know I saw her dancing there tonight, lithe and sexy and fluid and better than that first breath after nearly drowning, but I was too embarrassed and drunk to approach her and apologize and ask how she's been—to tell her I've missed her since she'd gone.

But here she is, a ghost, gliding toward me, as stunning

and shocking as ever, leaving me gobsmacked with bleary vision. Her red hair flips and flails behind her and she flickers in and out like a tired flame against a hard wind, the lights dimming and brightening along with her waning radiance, and when she reaches me she's angelic, ensconced in a burning white light, and she touches my face, torching it so that it melts off and falls like scalding soup into my lap. I scream and spill from the stool onto my back, the last breath knocked from me before I can suck it back in.

When my jarred and blackened vision clears, Old Man Bill's stooped over me, laughing, haloed in the bar's minimal overhead lighting, pulling his dentures in and out of his mouth and shoving them at my face, trying to fit them in my mouth. They smell like mustard and rotted cabbage and burnt coffee and shrimp left out in the sun. I feebly shove them away and try to stand but Old Man Bill's standing right over me, his yellow spittle misting me with each cackle. Darkness starts to consume the edges of my vision again until I'm staring through pinholes at Old Man Bill's flapping, wet lips. Then, absolute blackness.

Next thing I know, I'm in Old Man Bill's basement apartment on Ellis at Taylor in the Tenderloin district, just a few blocks from the bar, sitting beneath a dingy bare bulb illuminating only me, Old Man Bill, and the white Formica table baring a pattern of yellow daisies. In front of me a greasy plate of eggs and blackened potatoes quakes from Old Man Bill's sporadic cackles. The yolks are like two pools of oily, thick piss and I see my reflection in them, which shows me repeatedly winking at myself for some reason. Across from me, only a few feet away, Old Man Bill shovels strings of undercooked eggs into his mouth and slurps and licks at the corners of his mouth and throws his head back like a lizard swallowing a mouse whole. His adam's apple vibrates left to right. Then up and down. I notice he has taken his dentures out. They sit beside his plate in two pieces, yellow, but a darker yellow than the yolks and the daisies.

I push the plate away, stand up, and open the tiny, rectangular basement window to let in some of the night's black air. It smells like asphalt, burnt rubber, and diseased bowel movements. Undeterred, Old Man Bill immediately grabs my plate, mumbles, and starts forking those eggs and burnt taters into his maw, gnawing and mashing the potatoes with his gums. His floppy hat's hanging on a coat rack near the front door not too far away and I just now notice that he's got a full head of hair. Last I remember, though, he only had a bit of white behind the ears and around the lower back of his skull.

The place is mostly dark except for the yellow-brown dimness where we sit. The walls are concrete, white and cold. Painted white pipes snake along the tops of the walls and sometimes along the bottoms and disappear either into the walls, the floor, or ceiling. There's a constant hum from them interrupted only by the occasional flush and trickle of all the toilets situated right above his apartment.

The kitchen we're sitting in is just this table, an old red-brown refrigerator, and a folding table where there's a toaster and a microwave caked in the guts of exploded Hot Pockets and eggs. Squished golden cans of Hamm's litter the floor and table and glitter in the darkness like beach sand catching the last bit of moonlight.

Through the tiny basement window, I realize it's not all black night. In fact, it's a full moon and there's blue-white light pressing into the room, but it's swallowed quickly by the dingy bare bulb and the black hole Old Man Bill calls home. Old Man Bill, in between bites of oozing eggs, keeps looking up and out to where the moon would be, but the window's too small and the apartment's below ground. He sniffs at the moonlight in the air and scratches behind his left ear.

"What are we doing here, Bill?" I ask, sitting back down after pulling a Hamm's from a nearly empty 24-pack in his fridge.

Old Man Bill stops eating and slams his hands down hard onto the Formica table, causing the plates to clatter and making me flinch.

"How do you get a one-armed Polack out of a tree?" he asks, staring at me with his big wet blue eyes surrounded by pockets of sagging grey flesh.

"How'd I even get here, Bill?"

"Wave at him!" he says, losing his shit, tearing up from laughing so hard. Then he looks up at the window where the moonlight attempts to break in and howls and then looks back at me, wide-eyed, and laughs more toothless laughs. Silence follows until the silence is followed by scurrying sounds of small, many-legged creatures on the floor in the dark. Those sounds are obscured by the sounds of Old Man Bill getting up from the table and grabbing the plates. He tosses them into a large white tub that's clearly a utility sink and stained with lines and splatters of copper deposits and mildew.

"What are *you* doing here? What are you *doing* here?" he asks, his New Jersey accent thickening with the thickening hours of the night. "You dumb piece of shit."

Sipping from the warming Hamm's, I swallow back hard to keep from vomiting and say, "Yeah, what am I doing here?"

He shuffles over to me like Quasimodo, a dirty grey dishrag in his hand. He palms my skull with one fat, callused hand and pushes it back, spits on the rag and wipes at my forehead with rough jabbing and dragging motions. Turning the rag over and placing it in front of my face, he shows me the blood I guess I'd been bleeding. I must have hit my head pretty hard when Abigail burnt my face off.

In the dirty yellow light, Old Man Bill guffaws and slumps back down into his seat across from me and slams the dirty rag full of my blood down onto the Formica table sprouting daisies, real daisies now that quiver from the wind through the window and Old Man Bill's rotten breath.

Something grabs my thigh and bites and I jump and push away from the table and slam hard against the red-brown fridge, causing a picture frame to slip from its top and crash down at my feet. Before I can stoop, he's already there, picking the frame up and brushing bits of glass from the now dented, dinged, and ripped picture it holds. As he turns away I catch a glimpse of the child in it. It looks like a grade school class picture with a cheesy 70s backdrop replete with disco ball and laser lights. The kid's in a uniform of green pants and a white polo. His smile's gigantic and stupid and full of idiotic kid happiness that gets extinguished pretty soon after pictures like those are taken.

I realize the thing that clawed my leg was actually my phone vibrating and I pull it out and see a text from Sanchez saying he's at Aberdeen Tower and that I should pop by for a beer.

"It was bullshit, man," Sanchez says, putting his gin and tonic down on the bar so he can search frantically for his inhaler, bug-eyed and patting all over, frisking himself like an eager TSA agent. When he doesn't find it tucked away anywhere in his grey three-piece, he gets off his stool, lifts his grey metal suitcase onto it and pushes all his poetry papers and books around until he finds it. This is a pretty typical routine as he can never find anything like his inhaler or keys whenever he really needs them, and I'm growing pretty impatient, even while he's puffing medicine down into his clenching lungs and beginning to look a little more at ease. All I can think is, *Oxygen hates you, man. Just give up.*

"What? For fuck's sake, what's bullshit, Sanchez?" I ask,

taking a long pull on my Lagunitas IPA and staring him down.

"Anita. That fucking clown," he says, catching his breath and retaking his seat.

The angry Scottish bartender stalks past us behind the bar. He fills me with dread and reminds me of Michael Myers from *Halloween*, except he's not wearing a mask, he's just broad-shouldered and pale. Only difference is the chin-length brown hair he likes to let drop like drapes before his pale face, hiding himself in his own shadow. He passes by the TV replaying the Giants game from earlier tonight that I missed because of the Clap Your Hands Say Yeah show. He looks at me, grimaces, reaches up, and turns it off. I guess I should feel grateful for the half-inning I was able to watch.

"She's a clown, so what," I say, finishing off my Lagunitas and motioning to my friendly bartender that I'd like another. He slams it down in front of me, leans against the bar, stares me in the eyes, swipes my money from the bar, and slowly turns to deposit it into the clanging cash register.

"I know. I know it's her job," Sanchez says, sipping his gin and tonic, conceding that this is a fact and calming because of that concession. "But, shit, I didn't expect to find two balloons where her tits should be that say 'BLOW ME' on them when I finally got her top off. She's a carpenter's dream, man—flat as a fucking board."

An earth-shattering cackle erupts throughout the pub followed by a series of hands slapping and pounding the bar.

"Luke, why the fuck is Old Man Bill here with you?" Sanchez asks, sighing.

I look over at Old Man Bill who has suddenly grown a long grey beard and is still convulsing with laughter and I slap him on the shoulder. After a double-take, I reach over and tug on the beard to make sure it's real and laugh and slap him on the back once more.

"Old Man Bill here saved my life, Sanchez. I couldn't leave him all alone tonight after showing such bravery when staring down the Grim Reaper, face to face," I say, grinning like I can't help it.

"And what'd the Grim Reaper look like, exactly, you fucking crazy motherfuckers?" Sanchez asks as Old Man Bill's chuckles finally stifle behind his thickening, spittle-dewed beard.

"Actually, a lot like Abigail," I say.

"Abi-who?" Sanchez says, looking bored and definitely regretting inviting me to the Tower for a drink. Around us the bar buzzes with gossip and the flittering tongues of zombies lapping at thighs slick with the afterbirth of the stillborn.

"You remember—Abigail. The redhead? You danced with her that one time you, me, Gem, and that model you were dating crashed the Great American after hours and got shitfaced and danced to Janet Jackson and I stabbed the redhead and her boyfriend to death backstage," I say, taking big gulps of my beer while my eyes shift between Sanchez and the black TV screen.

"I seriously don't have a fucking clue what you're talking

about," he says and doesn't look at me.

I try to make eye contact but he refuses. I feel sick and sad. Like getting kicked in the gut. I just want confirmation that Sanchez remembers Abigail, too, and that she's not just a figment of imagination or cancerous memory. But, then I smell Old Man Bill's breath on my shoulder and push it back and decide not to be so scared or care so much.

Sanchez goes on to tell me how he hung out with some band at this fancy hotel down near Union Square and when I ask he tells me it was Clap Your Hands Say Yeah—how he bumped into them at the liquor store beneath his apartment and they invited him up to their hotel room to hang and that it was completely boring because there wasn't a single lady there and, while there was free coke that he's still in the midst of appreciating, that it was a complete waste of time. They were nerds, he says. Boring, he says. Geeks, he says. I tell him it's better than trying to fuck clowns and he says I'm probably right and stops complaining.

He's never heard of their band, however, and doesn't seem interested that I was at their show tonight with Kevin and his girlfriend and that I threw up a lot. I think to ask if he and Kevin are still friends since Kevin kicked him out of the apartment because Carol—the girlfriend—was moving in and didn't like him, but I decide to keep it to myself. He doesn't ask anything about them, either, and just tells me that he's still mad about me sleeping with that girl that looks like Cleopatra even though he wasn't interested in her because he was pursuing Anita, the clown. I tell him that while I slept with Cleopatra I didn't really, or that even if I did, I didn't, but that I don't think I did even if I had, and he doesn't get it and I'm not interested in explaining because I don't either and then he and I and Old Man Bill just sit there in silence for a while and sip our drinks and stare at the black TV.

"Ginger, ginger broke a winder, hit the winda—crack!" Old Man Bill says a little too loudly in the nameless divey shotgun bar a few blocks from Aberdeen Tower. We're here because it stays open after hours and doesn't enforce the no-smoking law.

"The baker came out to give him a clout…" he prattles on, "and landed on his back!" He cackles some more and slams his increasingly hairy hands against the bar, disturbing the fat, one-eyed lady 'tender who was actually very nice to us when we came in, offering us a free shot on the house as well as a wet kiss on each cheek, despite the fact that Old Man Bill's face is completely covered in hair now.

Unfortunately, I started this nonsense. I told Bill that he's an idiot for not loving baseball and Bill's going on about the things he loves: boxing, wrestling, tops, and knock down ginger. When I ask if that's all he loves, he looks at me with those blue eyes nearly hidden behind a face full of fur and tears up but doesn't say a thing. I pet his head and tell him he's good boy and he seems happy. I put a Sinatra song on the smoke-stained compact-disc jukebox because he's old and figure he'd like Sinatra. Hell, I like Sinatra. I play "My Way" and grab the furry bastard, who's all of five-foot-four, and dance him around the narrow place while the one-eyed, wart-faced bartender claps and laughs and wipes tears of joy from her eyes with the backs of her long-nailed pinkies. The other patrons, all of whom are missing limbs or parts of limbs or have grown extra limbs, seem less amused, but when I tell them he saved my life they thank him and congratulate him and feed him Milk Bones and shots of Old Crow. He laps at each and then offers to clean all empty glasses with his tongue only, which is now hairy, too. His offer's declined, and he tells them it's an open invitation and lets rip an excited howl.

I put on another Sinatra song and some Springsteen tunes and some Cash ballads and me, furry Old Man Bill, and the amputees while away the hours talking about nothing more important than the difference between a massage and a hand job, which has a lot of the regulars scratching their heads and demanding more clarity. Meanwhile, I avert my eyes from the TV because I'm always depressed by televisions in bars that play anything other than sports and on this TV is an old episode of *The Cosby Show* where the Cosbys catch Nancy Reagan doing coke and she cries and begs for their forgiveness and tells them how Ronald has a dick like a cat's penis—that it's barbed and every time he makes love to her she has to get restorative surgery performed on her pussy. I'm also pretty sure that's the episode where Rudy is upset because she hasn't learned to whistle yet. That's the part most people remember, I think.

They don't have the sound all the way off, however, so I hear Cash droning and mumbling and strumming while Nancy laughs wicked laughs every time Bill yells at one of the kids for leaving the refrigerator door open. I want to get out right then but Old Man Bill's now on all fours, covered from head to toe in fur, playing and padding around the blackened, sticky floor of the place, which is only a small swatch between the yellowed walls and bar that leads back to the yellowed bathrooms with doors that don't lock. The patrons have all gotten Old Man Bill into a game of fetch and not a one of them seems to want to stop it.

At 4 a.m. Old Man Bill sprints off on all fours and mauls a young man in a Matchbox 20 shirt at the corner of Stockton and Market, ripping out the guy's throat, so I have to put him on a leash. We move on from there and leave the kid bleeding out in the gutter and walk back toward Union Square, Old Man Bill furry as a sheepdog and panting like one, stopping here and there so he can lift his leg and mark his territory. He's grey, though, and his snout's longer than a sheepdog's. His teeth are like a shark's. Also, his paws look more like people hands, or maybe monkey or rat hands, and not dog paws. It doesn't matter, though, because he tells me I remind him of his son and I thank him and ask him about his son but doesn't want to say anything else. We take a seat on a bench at the square before the big glass-front of Macy's glistening in the light of the setting full moon. I pat Old Man Bill's dog-head and he pants and wags his tail, which is forked like a snake's tongue, but furry.

"What do you want for Christmas?" he asks, guttural and panting through a fat furry tongue.

"Don't even worry about it," I say. "It's not even close to Christmastime yet."

The early morning breeze passes through us, carrying a light scent of saltwater from the bay, and it's fresh and damp and new and covers the usual smell of blood and death and decay that weighs down the San Francisco fog, which is now nowhere to be seen.

"But a father should provide for his son," Old Man Bill says at the end of his leash. I reach into my pocket and pull out a Milk Bone and give it to him and then light up a Winston Light and sit back and smoke it in silence for a long time until the sky behind the buildings surrounding us starts to glow violet. Old Man Bill pants and wags his tail and fixes his gaze on me, waiting for a response. I drop my cigarette and try to avert my gaze, choosing to stare at the sunrise reflected in the windows of Macy's. I try to feel warmth, but I can't. The metal ball bearings tumbling through my veins crystallize and crack and fill me only with a million small stabbing sensations just below the skin. Scratching helps some, but there's no warmth to be found. I know there's sheets of fog curling and unfurling along the bay, grey and blue and coming straight for me. I want to be able to love this furry, mangy, smelly, old thing staring at me with expectation, wagging its tail and panting. I want to be able to connect with it and know it and relate to it. It saved my life, after all, which is not too dissimilar from giving me life in the first place.

And then Old Man Bill barks and walks a circle three times before lying on the concrete at my feet with his hairy, misshapen head resting over his crossed legs or arms. He mumbles, sleepily, again, that I remind him of his son and closes his eyes and drifts to a seemingly contented sleep, his long tongue dangling out the side of his muzzle.

"Dog!" I shout excitedly and reach down to rub Old Man Bill's furry head but the sun's come up over the buildings to make everything grey and ugly and Old Man Bill is at my feet, ugly and wrinkled and reeking and old and the same as always—just curled up at my feet, quiet and cold and still and bald and toothless—no longer furry or able to play fetch with anything except pint glasses in dark bars, hoping to be rewarded with free drinks and the young's placating amusement. And in bars I call my own. In spaces I go to be alone and hope to never return from.

"Dog!" I say again before kicking him in the toothless mouth as the sound of buses, cars, and zombies, rising with the sun, starts to churn on every side of Union Square. His mouth turns red and drips and I don't care. Planes fly overhead and explode and I don't care. People stumble below the wheels of buses and split in two, geysers of blood erupting from their unzippered skin and splashing organs, and I don't care. He doesn't move before or after the kick and I don't care. So I kick him a couple more times, and anyone that sees simply averts their gaze and moves on, and Old Man Bill barely registers the blows, his eyes open, unblinking, distant and lost and I don't care. I go home where I take a shower and dress and forget about yesterday so that I can start another day and I don't care.

CLEOPATRA

Some for-shit's-sake Oasis song plays overhead followed by a Christ-please-split-my-head-open Dave Matthews song, and my head is already aching enough from the hangover and lack of sleep as Sanchez and me wait for his date to show up, standing on the mezzanine of Aberdeen Tower, a Scottish bar on Geary down the street from Bourbon Bandits where I usually waste my time.

The bar smells of stale dishwater pooled underneath rubber floor mats. It's lit in a dim, hazy orange hue. Looking down from the mezzanine, past little flags of the Lion Rampant strung between the two upper levels, I see Kevin all gangly with hair disheveled chatting up a cute blonde named Christy that I work with at a café in Hayes Valley. He's drunk and pretending he's only accidentally touching her tits as she giggles. The Giants and Dodgers game is on the bulky TV behind them but no one is watching so no one sees the ballplayers, in unison, like synchronized swimmers, reach deep into their jockstraps and retrieve tiny pistols which they quickly slip between their lips. As they pull the triggers, their heads explode into tiny flakes of red confetti and their bodies collapse in unison as dozens of dancers and cheerleaders tumble and cartwheel onto the dirt diamond and perform a dramatic interpretive dance to Leonard Cohen's "Hallelujah" while the umpires confer in front of home plate and chat calmly between sips of whiskey from a shared flask. Then the umpires agree to remove the headless figures and confetti, getting to the task of tugging bodies away and sweeping just before the song ends, the dancers depart, and the first car commercial graces the TV screen.

"What's she look like, again?" I ask Sanchez who often refers to his own looks as a cross between Johnny Depp and Gomez Addams. He's in a grey three-piece suit, as usual, and fidgeting, as usual.

"She looks like fucking Cleopatra," he says through pained exhaustion, searching his pockets and pulling out an inhaler and taking a quick hit before scanning the crowd. "Only, not quite as skinny."

"Was Cleopatra skinny?" I ask.

"Yeah. She got fit building the goddamned pyramids," Sanchez says.

He pulls out a cigarette then remembers there's no smoking allowed in the bar. The jukebox quiets for a second and I hear Kevin yelling to Christy, "No, seriously, it's my real fucking hair!" with a huge shit-eating grin on his face, and then the CD changes and New Order's "Ceremony" plays and I quit listening to Sanchez complaining about how he would prefer to leave, how his hair is not quite right, and that he needs to take a shit anyway and should just go.

Instead, I listen to the song and sing along in my head and watch Kevin flirt with Christy, who's all smiles, touching his arm from time to time, and I try to forget my relentless crush on her even though she's kind of a hippie.

She's sweet, though. She gave me a black candle and mixed CD for my 27th birthday, although I could not listen to the hippie drum-circle garbage she filled the CD with more than once. I only use it to set my drinks on or cut lines of coke now, but I think of her every time I see it and feel pretty good about it. The black candle has come in handy with late night drunken hookups, and each time I let a thick, black liquid bead spill onto an erect nipple or the inside of an already-reddened thigh, I think of her and wish she was with me instead.

She has a soft face, too—one that's full of forgiveness for things that haven't even been done yet. She has these bright blue eyes, and these flushed cheeks. She's nice. She looks nice. When I think of her, I think: *nice*. I like thinking about her. I do it often.

For a second I think about going down the stairs, ditching Sanchez and decking Kevin, but then I hear Sanchez say, "Shit. There she is," and I look back and down toward the front of the bar and there's Cleopatra with picture-perfect bangs, draped in a short black dress, taking a table with a few other girls. She's gorgeous and full of self-importance and completely in control of her surroundings. Her friends are on invisible leashes and they're all bats and lashes toward her.

"Shit!" I hear Sanchez say again. He looks all around at the green bugs with big glowing asses and long sharp teeth that swarm around us at this moment. He swats at them, makes a face like he's smelling something awful, and pulls out another cigarette before remembering again and putting it back. Then he finds his inhaler and takes another puff on that and adjusts his tie and asks how his hair is. I say "fine" then turn around again to take another look at Cleopatra and when I turn back Sanchez is shimmying down the stairs and I figure he must be on his way to say hello but he keeps on down the stairs then toward the back of the bar where the restrooms are and, instead of going into the men's room, he takes the backdoor out into the alleyway. That heavy metal door slams silently behind him amidst the cheers from the three or four at the bar cheering on the Giants game.

Sanchez does not, in fact, have a change of heart and bust back through that metal door to more canned applause. Instead, I can see him—in my head, only—waltzing down the alleyway in a Charlie Chaplin-esque strut, laughing to himself. Then he doubles over with that laughter before moving along, high-fiving the rats in the alleyway who all compliment his suit before scratching their balls and shoving their faces back into the dumpster or another rat's ass.

He's ditched out on so many hopeful and adoring women by now that it's become a predictable yet constant source of amusement for most of his friends. Mostly it annoys me. The dismissal he shows women without a second's thought is something I'm completely incapable of.

Suddenly abandoned and surrounded by gaseous bugs and odiferous hippies talking about Colonel Sanders' unforgivable sins—while masturbating each other under the tables with one hairy-palmed hand and picking at their dreads with the other—I decide to walk down and interrupt Kevin and Christy's coitus.

"What's up, shitbag?" I say to Kevin, squeezing in between the two and ordering myself a vodka-soda from the aloof and mostly pissed-off Scottish bartender. He looks at me, wordless, makes no gesture, then gets to the work of laboring over my order.

"Hi, Luke!" Christy says, drinking her cosmo with a straw. I notice a daisy planted behind her right ear and I wonder what kind of soil she must have inside her skull that it would grow so brightly.

"Um, hey," I say, then turn my back to her. "Sanchez split. Pulled his usual out-the-back-door antics."

"Eh, what are ya gonna do?" Kevin asks, trying to see around me but I masterfully block his view of Christy's smallish frame.

The friendly barkeep returns with my drink and I see that the Giants are losing 12 to nothing now. I take my drink, drop six bucks on the bar and point to the TV, "Fucking typical, right?" The bartender, saying nothing, turns, looks at the TV, turns back to me and takes the money. He switches the TV off with three innings left in the game as he walks back to the cash register.

"Real fucking gentleman," I say to Christy and as her mouth starts to form a response I turn my back on her again and say, "So, what the fuck, Kevin?"

"What, Luke?" Kevin asks, tired. Suddenly everyone in the bar sags with fatigue and the bugs take the opportunity to crawl into their ears. No one has the energy to swat them away. Everyone in the bar starts buzzing in a monotonous opera for 10 seconds. Then they stop.

"Do you believe this shit?" I say, again looking at Christy who gives me a puzzled look as we all slip out of our momentary but musical malaise.

"Listen," I say to Christy. "What's going on here?" The TV behind me flashes violently between violet, blue, and red before going black again.

"Um, I, uh, don't know what you're talking about, Luke," Christy says, her cheeks more flushed than normal.

I look back at Kevin who only looks bored.

"What the fuck are you doing here with Kevin?" I say as I recall a time during a lull in the work day at Café Communisto when Christy and I had snuck down to the basement for a quick fuck and I tore her shirt right off her, tore it to so many shreds she had to wear my undershirt the rest of the day, nearly disappearing in it.

Then I try to remember if that actually happened even though I can easily recall the menthol warmth of her Burt's Bees lip balm on my own lips—can recall with crystal clarity that her thighs were small, tight, smooth, and smelled like peppermint when I grabbed them and spread them and put my face against them.

"Luke?" Christy says, snapping a finger in front of my face. I notice my drink is gone and the TV is back on and *Braveheart* is playing, but in ultra-slow motion. Mel Gibson's enormous head and jaw slide from left to right and his eyes don't blink and overhead The Smiths are saying, "William, it was really nothing," and I picture this bar in the middle of a Shakespeare play where the bartender gets drawn and quartered, Kevin gets poisoned, and I exit on a two-headed horse with Cleopatra and Christy in chains behind me, tied to the horse, only to find out all that really happened was that I accidentally slept with Oedipus.

"What?" I say. "Wait, what? What was I talking about?"

I order another drink and Christy says, "You said you were thinking of going to visit your mom, which I think is really sweet. You haven't seen her in a while, have you?"

"What?"

"You haven't seen her recently, right? Anyway, I think it's a great idea. If you can forgive your mom, and I think you should, really, then that's great. Go see her this weekend and patch things up."

As I look at Christy her blue eyes turn into neon pools of moonlit perfection and it makes my heart actually ache to look at her before I say, "Mind your own fucking business. Jesus, who the fuck do you think you're talking to?" and Kevin already has his hands on my shoulders pulling me away and I push him back against the bar and when his back hits the bar the TV flashes back to the Giants game just long enough to see that they came back to win the game 13 to 12, which gives me two seconds of rare hope, then it goes back to Mel Gibson and both Christy and Kevin are giving me a look I don't understand and my head hurts so I ask them if they have any Advil and they both tell me to fuck off which I don't get and my eyes go watery and it's all I can do to keep from crying and I start thinking about the time Christy and I went to the Legion of Honor and dumbly stared at Rembrandts and portraits of Jesus in orgies with 11 other men and one prostitute before heading out to the nearby golf course to sit on a bench and share my flask of whiskey and make out madly before all the bright green grass as the Pacific lay blue and cold beneath a hill behind us.

Suddenly something clicks in me and I reach between Kevin and Christy for my drink and walk back toward the front of the bar where Cleopatra sits with her two friends.

"Sanchez isn't gonna show up," I say, interrupting some heated discussion about acrylic nails versus the real thing and where to get a really good facial.

Cleo looks up and without skipping a beat says, "Yeah, Luke, I'm well aware of that. I saw him hightail it out the back way. I don't get him. I really don't."

"How do you know me, again? I mean, how do you know my name?"

"Luke," she says. "Luke. Are you fucking kidding me? Luke. Are you fucking *kidding* me?"

Next I know, she's up from the table and standing next to me, looking up at me with dark eyes moving all over my face with a hint of pity. I figure the green bugs are probably still following me. I then see one of those bugs in a Giants cap that I named Jim some time ago because he reminds me of a fake uncle I once had. Jim gives Cleo the finger then nosedives into a glass of Jim Beam at the bar.

"You obviously need another drink, Luke," she says, noticing my empty glass. She then drags me to her table and seats me next to her, her two friends on the other side of the table awaiting any clue that it's okay for them to inquire or join in the conversation. Before they can, Cleo hails a waitress with a queen's persistence and sets me up with a Grey Goose and soda water.

"So, Luke, what's his problem? I mean, seriously?"

"Wait… how do you know me?"

"Shut the fuck up, Luke. Enough of the jokes. What's with Sanchez? He's so suave it's disgusting but he runs away almost every time we're supposed to meet up. It's not cool."

"Wait, you two know each other, too?"

"Boy, you really are a dolt, aren't you?" she asks, knocking on my head and making hollow sounds out of her beautifully formed mouth.

Her friends are glassy-eyed and looking back and forth between me and Cleo with a kind of irrepressible anticipation and I'm pretty sure one is drooling.

"You need another drink," Cleo says and I don't think I've had a chance to say a word let alone take a drink but when I look down I see my empty glass and she's ordering me another and she has her arm around me. For some reason she's making me feel like the center of attention, even though it's clear that she is. As far as I can tell, she's completely forgotten about her friends staring at us bug-eyed with awe and envy.

The fresh drink arrives and then Mel Gibson dies and everyone in the bar cries violent, eye-exploding tears, and Cleo is grabbing my thigh while Kevin is consoling Christy from the tragic, dramatic, and upsetting loss of Mel Gibson in face paint.

"You need another drink," Cleopatra says yet again and the jukebox is on "Love Will Tear Us Apart" for the twelfth time tonight. Again, I don't remember finishing my last vodka she ordered, but, again, the glass is as dry as southern California and my vision is blurry and I'm pretty sure Kevin now has his hand up Christy's shirt and she has hers down his pants and I can't understand why she's doing this to me, after the moments we had together, those moments that could have added up to mean something larger than the both of us, and now she's making a fool of me to my face pretending none of that ever happened or meant a goddamned thing.

Then I remember the Giants came back tonight from a complete and bloody annihilation (that 12 to 0 deficit) and before I know it the next drink Cleo buys for me is here then gone and the next is just the same and her friends are shooed away and my hands are on her thighs and breasts and my lips are pressed hard against hers and she's making the small wounded sounds of pleasure.

Standing outside on Geary Street we kiss more in the haze of the street lights, up against Aberdeen Tower's front windows, her ass pressed magnificently up against that glass before deciding she'll come to my place tonight, which is just a block or two around the corner and up the city hill.

As we're about to leave, I see Sanchez in the window of the second story apartment right across from Aberdeen Tower where he rooms with Kevin. Sanchez is staring at me while Christy and Kevin grope each other off to his side. I see him on his phone and get a text that interrupts Cleo's wandering hands and the text says, "So now you're interested in her? You fucking prick."

I look up at Sanchez and laugh and lead Cleopatra by the hand back to my place. When in my brightly lit jail cell of a studio-apartment I quickly undress her after putting on a CD by The Church. The song "Reptile" beats against my close walls as I bury my face in her pussy and fall asleep for two minutes or so and wake up to Cleo saying, "Here, take a bump," to my protests of, "I don't do coke. I've never done coke. No. I don't think so. I don't do coke. It'll give me a fucking heart attack or something. I've never done it," and she reassures me, "You'll be fine, but you may not be able to get it up. Just stay the fuck awake and finish what you started," and she pulls out a tiny Ziploc bag from her humungous purse, grabs her keys, dips in and shoves it up her nose before doing it again and offering it to me.

"Oh, I'll be able to get it up, don't worry about that," I say and take the bump and feel the familiar return to near-normalcy where the room warms from its invisible center to glow in a blur around its edges. Then the walls close in and my heart nearly explodes before I realize Cleo is already tied up to the bed posts with my black tie, her wrists bound together, her bronzed ass reddened, her long jet black hair matted against her perfect back glistened with sweat while a loud, obnoxious Terra Patrick porn plays on my little TV and The Church keeps going on about milky ways and blood money.

As I'm fucking Cleopatra I'm thinking about Christy and that time we went to that Yo La Tengo concert at the Fillmore and how we left halfway through, catching a cab back to my apartment to drink wine and dance and screw for hours with the windows open to let the warm air and city sounds blow in. The next day we woke up groggy and tired-eyed but happy and went to work at the café together where we pretended nothing happened, which only made the work day more exciting.

I really can't understand what went wrong there.

Cleo is shoving more coke up my nose, eternally grateful to be untied, speaking to me in hot-breathed words with a tight body ready to turn to jelly at my slightest touch.

I push her advances away as something in my stomach goes bad. I get off the bed, turn the porn off and switch The Church to The Rapture and look around my computer desk for my phone.

"Luke, what the fuck?" Cleo says, sighing, falling back into bed, glittering like Mediterranean sands.

"Shut up," I say, finding my phone.

"Excuse me?"

"Shut the fuck up! I'm trying to concentrate."

Desperately I search through the contact list in my phone, trying to find Christy's number as I suddenly have a million things to say to her, to tell her. Things like, I'm sorry I didn't appreciate her, that I wish the moments we had could have been more and that I still think about the times we had all the time and that I'm thinking about them right now and if we could just talk maybe we could work things out and that Kevin is not the guy for her and how could she be fucking one of my friends, anyway, it's completely uncalled for, and that if I thought about it maybe I'm in love with her and everything *is* my fault.

While scrolling through my phone, confused, unable to find Christy's fucking number I look back at Cleopatra who is getting fucked by a rather large cricket and seemingly enjoying it more than she should. Then a rat scurries over my foot and I give up and go back to Cleo, shove the shiny, dark thing from her, gather up the sand she's made of, push it back into a form I can recognize, and fuck her until the sun rises.

In the light of that sunrise, I stand before my lone window and watch a falcon perched on the fire escape grasp a pigeon in its talons and beat it to death with its beak in a kick-drum-like rhythm while Cleo snores softly, just a few feet behind me on the futon.

I make coffee on the hot plate, my head in a cloud, my body in a complete state of arrest, full of anxiety and tension. Cleo wakes up, all smiles.

"What's going on?" she asks.

"I'm making coffee."

"Yeah?"

"Yeah."

"Pour me a cup, please," she says, sitting up, stretching into illumination until she's only a few beams of scattered light.

"If you'd like a cup of coffee, there's a café up on the corner of Stockton," I say, my back to her.

"Are you fucking kidding me?"

"I don't even fucking know you. Just, you know, show yourself out," I say, making a comical gesture embellishing the size of my shithole studio apartment.

"So, after all that, this is what it comes to? You tossing

me out of your place?" she asks, getting out of bed, pulling on her panties, searching for her bra, eyeing me the whole time.

"Yes," I say, sipping too-hot and bitter coffee, watching pigeon feathers flood the air outside the window like a tickertape parade for the soon-to-be dead.

"One night. That's all you get, sweetheart."

"One fucking night? Jesus, you are a bigger prick than I thought. One fucking night? Really? *Really*? One fucking night? What about that time at the museum? Have you forgotten about that? The way we connected back then? How we kissed so hard on that park bench that you said you could still taste my lip balm the next day? Seriously? Don't you ever think about the times we've had together? It wasn't that long ago, Luke. How can you just forget all about me? I thought you were kidding when you asked me how I knew you, but now you're scaring me. What about that time I visited you at your café and there was no one there so we snuck down to the basement and fucked? You can't recall that, either, huh? What about that concert where you couldn't get enough of me and we left early so we could drink wine and fuck and dance and be alone together? Any of this ringing a bell, asshole? How about that fucking time I went with you to visit your goddamned sick mother that you hadn't spoken to in, what, five fucking years? Luke, seriously. Are you fucking kidding me? One fucking night is all I get? I only went after Sanchez to try to get your attention, you fucking asshole! Did you not get that? Christ, what a fucking dick you are!" she says before throwing something like an ax at me that splits my head in two, splattering dark red blood against all four walls of my studio.

Then she walks out.

After she leaves, I clean up my walls with wet rags, using slow, meticulous circular motions, going clockwise, then counter-clockwise. Then I suture my skull together with a sewing kit I bought from Walgreens, wincing with each piercing but refusing to let my eyes tear up. I used it only once before to repair a six-inch crevice that opened spontaneously in the left side of my torso a year earlier. When I've finished cleaning the walls and tying my skull together it's 10 a.m., so, I go to Jack in the Box with an empty head and wait in line with the zombies to get something to eat.

FATHERHOOD

Gurgling. Orange curtains billowing. A metallic scent. More gurgling. A sticky wood floor. Green walls. I lift my left all-black Chuck Taylor All-Star and it makes a suction-smacking sound. Gurgling. I don't know where I am. I don't know what day it is. Orangish morning light waves in with the orange billowing curtains. My stomach feels green, like sick and bloated and hurt. Like, I ate something that wants to eat me. I lift my right all-black Chuck Taylor All-Star and it makes a suction-smacking sound. The Winston I forgot in my right hand burns to the filter and singes my end-knuckles. Instinctively, I flick it away. It goes out with a slick fizzle.

Gurgling. There's an unmade bed next to the window with billowing orange curtains. A boxy TV in the corner of the room plays a beer commercial showing bikini-clad ladies in snow-clad mountains. They keep yelling, screaming, pleading in a foreign language while shivering and rubbing their arms. Only, it's muted. Their mouths move, nothing comes out. A close-up of goosebumps on what is either boob or ass cleavage or a pair of elbows. It changes views before we can tell. Cartoon speak-bubbles eschew from their lips and read, "Enjoy me!". The speak-bubbles flash and flicker in and out and in a wide spectrum of colors. Then the commercial ends and turns to static. Then it flickers back to the commercial and everyone's head is snapping back and forth off their shoulders like the heads of Pez dispensers. A bloody lozenge falls out each time. A bearded man in filthy, street-oil-stained clothing crawls through the snow around the bikini-clad girls and retrieves the bloody lozenges and slides them into his anus like suppositories. The camera closes in on his big, bearded, grinning face. I get it. It's a constipation commercial. It has nothing to do with beer. I feel stupid for a second. The commercial bleeds into another for handlebar mustache wax that doubles as lube.

Gurgling. Horns and morning traffic and grumpy zombies grunt and fart and moan outside, their noise coming inside with the orange curtains and orange light.

Gurgling. My hands are sticky. When I press them together, or open and close a fist, they make the same suction-smacking sound my all-black Chuck Taylor All-Stars do. There's something familiar about this. Like, I dreamed it. My head hurts, though, the way it hurts when I haven't slept well, or at all. Pulsing and bulging and aching, like my brain has a dry erection.

Gurgling. The orange morning breeze off of Geary Street

soothes me some, though the scent of bloody feces and burnt coffee that it carries only hurts my green stomach more. I stare down at the butt of my Winston on the floor. It's all black and sticky. Like my All-Stars. I squish my fingers into my palms—suction-smacking sounds. Like my All-Stars. I do it again. And again. And again. I click my teeth and flitter my eyelashes, but nothing comes into complete focus.

Gurgling. Someone calling for their momma. A metallic scent. A tingle in my dick. Like, static electricity. It tickles. I laugh but don't touch or scratch my junk. Instead, I pat my dress-shirt pocket for my pack of Winstons. My black skinny tie dangles loosely. My sleeves are rolled up. I tighten the tie and unroll my sleeves and nearly choke on the smell in the room. I mask the smell of quick-rot by lighting up a cigarette and blowing smoke into the space around me. It turns the green walls brown and my green stomach blue. I feel sad. And I know why.

Gurgling. I look down at my feet. I see my all-black Chuck Taylor All-Stars. A few inches from them, I see Cameron's big brown eyes rolling all over the place. Cameron's choking on her own blood. But just barely as she's nearly out of her own blood. Her brown hair is black. It's gross. It's matted and sticky and dark. She doesn't smell good. It's upsetting. I feel my blue stomach go green again and nearly vomit. I nearly shit myself and wish I hadn't taken those suppositories. But I don't. I realize what's happening, though I don't understand how or why. I hurt. More than just my stomach, now. I feel sick and sad.

Gurgling. I lean down and say, "Cameron, sweetie, what happened?"

But, she's too sticky and self-involved to answer.

I try again, "Baby, what's wrong? What can I do?"

Again, too proud to tell me. I should have known this would happen. I've loved Cameron for a couple years now, though she rarely paid me any mind. I frequented the bar she tended, Bourbon Bandits, regularly, convinced she'd finally notice me. She never did. No matter how many times I jumped up on the bar after seven pints of whiskey and soda water and sang along to Duran Duran's "Come Undone," it didn't matter. I would tell her I never dance for anyone unless I'm in love, or drunk, and she would ignore me and ask me to leave. I would tell her I love her and that I'm not scared of the monster tattooed on her arm—or leg, or tit, or back, or wherever it is these days. I just wasn't scared of it anymore. I got over it. It took months of living in a black room, but her monster didn't scare me. I knew we all had it under control. She had it under control. I had it under control. We all had it under control. And, besides, monsters aren't real. That's just stupid. Only stupid people believe in monsters.

She knew I loved her, though. She wasn't stupid. No. She told me she knew once after I bought her a few shots and no one else but Old Man Bill was in the bar at the end of the night. She said, "I know you're in love with me, loser." She said, "Love is for suckers, idiot." She said, "My vagina's eight feet wide."

I felt inadequate.

Old Man Bill was collecting empties and glasses and bringing them to her in exchange for a free drink on the morrow. Crickets kept dropping from his hairy ears and from the holes in his smile.

Despite that, every once in a while I, or one of the other regulars, would buy him a drink, too. Like a pigeon, he kept coming back to the source. Despite all the signs around town that said "Don't Feed the Old Man Bills" we felt good about ourselves for doing the opposite. One night, after making a tasteless comment about the one black girl in the bar, he told us he might just punch our faces off. Then he laughed a toothless laugh and we poured a couple whiskeys down his throat. We hoped he'd die of liver failure right there, but God doesn't work that way. He's lazy and not at all interested in offing those that really deserve it. Like Old Man Bill. What a piece of shit, right?

Gurgling. "Shhh," I say, petting her blood-blackened brown hair away from her bloodshot eyes. "Shhh, sweetie, just tell me who did this to you."

She says something like, "Call an ambulance," but I'm simply too upset to really get at what she means.

"Shhh," I say. "Just… just stay calm. I'm here, baby. I'm here."

I'm holding her head with both hands. I bellow, "No!" when her eyes flicker and seem about ready to go out. I yell out, "Shit!" when her blood-soaked hair puts out my Winston. I gently lay her head back down in the pool of black sticky blood and look for my cigarettes again. Opening the pack, I find I'm fresh out.

"Fucking great," I say. "Listen, honey—Cameron—I have to go out and get some more cigarettes. I'll be right back, okay?"

But, as I should expect, her eyes stop moving all together. They slide over to the right and stop. I can't fathom what she's even looking at over there. From her vantage point, all she could possibly be looking at is the dust and lost cigarette butts and crumbs of pizza crust stuck under the nightstand next to her bed.

"Baby," I say. "There's nothing there." I gently slap the side of her face, "There's nothing there." My sticky hand sticks to her sticky face and it pulls away with a Velcro-like sound. "There's nothing there," I repeat, more resolutely.

Crumpling up the empty golden Winstons box, I take a deep breath and throw it into the trash bin next to the nightstand. "I'll be right back, baby," I tell Cameron, who's still playing coy.

I'm not completely stupid, of course. I know what's going on. I didn't go to San Francisco State University and get a degree just because I paid for it. I'm a smart guy. A sensitive guy. I'm upset. I'm in shock. I'm lots of things.

So, I exit the room and try to remember if I have $7.75 in my bank account in order to buy a fresh pack of Winstons. I'm not sure, so I return to Cameron and ask if I can borrow a tenner.

She doesn't say anything, so I riffle through her pockets, roll her over, and find a wad of her tip money tucked into her back pants pocket. I tell her thanks and slip the cash into my front pants pocket. I say I'll pay her back soon as I can the way I always do when she hands money off to me.

When I'm opening the front door of Cameron's apartment in the Tenderloin on Geary, a high-tide of scents from the hallway floods my senses: moldy carpets, wood rot, old piss, bloody feces, body odor, stale beer, nickels and dimes, and yellow-green phlegm.

It's enough to knock me back, though I don't know why I haven't grown used to it. San Francisco is a festering, red-ringed and pus-filled wound dressed up like a cheap postcard. Its legs are open to all, except those of color or lack of funds. Now that I think about it, why the disenfranchised and disallowed don't do worse than piss and shit and bleed all over its pretend-beauty, I don't know. In fact, I'm so overcome with solidarity that I whip my dick out and piss a thick stream of steaming yellow piss right into the hallway of Cameron's apartment building. As an unemployed white man, I'm right there with the rest that the system has totally fucked over. When I flick the last yellow drops from the tip of my dick, I raise a fist and yell, "Power to the people!"

Cigarettes. Fuck, I need cigarettes.

Then, "Momma?"

The pitter-patter of feet as dirty as freshly pulled

potatoes.

Zipping up I turn back into Cameron's apartment and see Toby stumbling out of his bedroom and rubbing his eyes.

"Momma?" it says again.

"Hey there, little guy," I say, heading him off at the pass. I can hear the orange curtains in the other room billowing in with the orange morning light.

"Lou?" the potato-head says, pulling his little fist away from his eye. He's three or six or ten—how the fuck am I supposed to know?

"Uh, it's Luke, kid," I say and muss his potato-head mop.

"Lou?" it says again.

"Sure, yeah. Okay. I'm Lou. Alright. Look, Toby, your ma—she's sleepy. Real tired, okay? I'm gonna take care of you today," I say and pinch his fat potato-y cheek.

"You a take me to school?" it says, eyes wide. Cameron's stench from the other room is becoming unbearable. I grab the kid by the hand and pull him out the door and pull the door closed behind us before he can smell her foul disrespect.

"School?" I ask, kneeling down to make eye contact with it because I remember being told that little monsters like to bring you down to their level in order to communicate clearly. "Do you really go to school? Or are you playing pretend?"

"Hungy," it says and rubs its eyes before holding its arms out to me.

Down the building's hallway, I hear Cameron's sister

jostling with the locks of her own apartment door. Quickly, I pick the kid up and skip down the piss-wet stairs.

"What, you don't like it?" I ask, nudging the little guy in the ribs as I slice up the ham on my plate. The cheap boombox in the corner plays Blink 182's cover of Spice Girls' cover of Ace of Base's cover of Ugly Kid Joe's cover of "Cat's in the Cradle".

We're at Golden Coffee, a tiny corner diner at Stockton and Leavenworth. It has big windows, and a square horseshoe counter, and that's it. It's about a block uphill. I like to come here early in the morning and watch the refuse of the previous night roll down the hill: wallets, spare trolley wheels, Prada bags, the hopes and dreams of privileged people sunk by a bad break. Those dreams usually look like Britney Spears as they come tumbling down the hill, but end up looking like Fed Savage in high heels at the bottom of it. Each time it happens, I'm embarrassed. Embarrassed because I always run out after the messy tumbling mass and yell, "Britney, I'll save you!" but in the end Fred wants nothing to do with me and just raises one eyebrow at me while giving me a look of disgust before hobbling up Geary toward Union Square to drink out of the bowls there that catch rainwater and are labeled with names such as "Fido" or "Mayor".

"Is greezy," the kid says, handling his utensils like a fucking Neanderthal.

"Greasy?" I ask, exasperated. "This is what's called a

greasy spoon diner, son. Here, I'll cut this up for you. There, now eat. It's good for you. Makes you shit. That's good for you I hear. I sort of read a book about it once. Keeps the ass cancer away." I gulp down my coffee and motion to the old Asian guy that runs the place that I'd like another, please. He smiles and refills my stained and chipped mug while his slightly younger brother works behind a sizzling grill at the back of the counter next to the industrial-sized sink full of bubbles. Just then, I feel inspired and pen a poem onto a napkin:

Golden Coffee
how I love thee so
let me count the ways:
your coffee
bacon
and eggs
are the tops
but you're so much more
than a greasy spoon to me
your hash browns
rye toast
and counter service
are also pretty neat
and I think the cook's name is Fred
which is also kinda neat
Golden Coffee
your view of the busy intersection
and pedestrian traffic
is pretty sweet
Golden Coffee
how I love thee
you're one swell place to eat

Then I fold the napkin up and slip it into the shirt pocket where my Winstons should be. I smile, knowing the poetry community will eat it up and praise me, but give me no money. Speaking of, I plan to pay for this meal with the money I stole out of the tip jar from the fancy café across the street.

"Yeah?" I say, nudging the kid in the ribs again. He groans and moans and pouts and leans away from me. "What? You don't like their breakfast? Look, these people here worked very hard to make that ham and eggs for you. And I have it on good authority that you've read a book called *Green Eggs and Ham*—you know what they call this? Living the experience, son. Now, eat up."

"I did a read dat book," it says, handling his fork and knife like an invalid.

"Hey, now!" I say. "I told you I knew you, you little bugger, you. Now, chow down. In this meal you'll get most of the nutrients you need to grow into a full-grown man—primarily, pig nutrients."

To show him there's nothing wrong with slimy diner food, I greedily chop up my own ham and eggs and shovel it into my face. He smiles. So, I start shoveling faster. His smile turns to giggles. I take it to the next level because I'm sleep deprived—and sad and confused and sickened about Cameron, I think—and pick up the plate and start gobbling at it like a cow at a trough. That has the little shit grabbing at his stomach and laughing so hard that he falls off the stool.

***

"Can I hold-a your hand, pawleez?" it asks as we're walking down Geary, our bellies full of greasy ham and eggs and goodness.

"*Can* you hold my hand?" I ask. "Of course you *can*."

The little dummy holds his hand out and wiggles his little digits. I don't take his hand.

"You a said you hol' my hand," it says, pouting again and looking like it's about to cry.

"See, this is why I'm here," I tell Toby, kneeling down again so that we make eye contact. While I'm preparing my response, Geary Street's usual zombies and monsters walk past, bumping into me while scratching the sores on their faces and crotches. One walks right into me, trips over my back, and slams into the concrete. It makes the sound of a mallet swung hard into a side of beef. He doesn't get up, and I don't bother to offer help. Toby looks at him and erupts into giggles.

"I'm here," I say over his laughter, "to show you how to grow the fuck up. You *can* hold my hand. What you meant to ask was, '*May* I hold your hand?'. You understand? You see the fucking difference?"

"I'm five. You us't a bad word. I am not growed up, you know," he says, pouting again.

"Jesus! I know that. I *am* growed up. Are you listening?"

I grab his hand and we walk down the sidewalk littered with needles and used condoms and lost teeth. Kicking those aside, we eventually end up at Bourbon Bandits.

Stan's behind the bar skittering around on his skinny cricket legs. As usual, there's no one here, but the bartender seems busy as shit. A high-pitched whistle, barely audible, accompanies his every move.

I pick up potato-head and place him on the bar.

"Oh, uh, hi, Luke," Stan says in the midst of utter confusion. "What—you taking care of Toby today?"

"That's what it looks like," I say, and take a seat at the bar. On one of the TVs the Giants' pregame show has begun. On the other, a man wearing an American-flag dress is spreading George W. Bush's legs and tonguing his asshole.

"Stan," I say.

"Huh?" he asks, looking up from his glass-washing duties.

"You think that's appropriate for children to be seeing?" I ask, pointing at the rimjob taking place on the TV.

Stan stares at the TV and asks, "What? The news? Shelter the kid much?"

"Don't look at that," I say, covering the thing's eyes, though he's busy playing with a Transformers toy Stan must have given him. "You're too young to be bothered with politics," I finish, but realize he's too interested in his toy, so I take my hand from his eyes. I can't help but think there's something symbolic happening.

"Stan, give me the usual, *pour a favor*," I say, having a hard time taking my eyes off the TV that isn't showing the Giants' pregame.

"Wha's that?" it asks, pointing now at that TV.

"The way the world goes 'round. Don't look at it, kid. It'll make you sick. Jesus, Stan, you really can't turn that shit off?" I ask, putting my hand over the kid's eyes again. "I'm trying to raise a child here, man. He doesn't need to see that shit."

Outside: sirens, flashing lights, screams, the smell of bacon with a side of gunfire.

Stan pays no mind to anything but his precious glasses that must be cleaned and cleaned and cleaned. Finally, after washing a thousand glasses and stopping before the mirror to comb the mustache masking his flittering mandibles, he walks over and says, "The usual, Luke. Really?"

"Exprechen eee doytch?" I ask. "Yeah, the usual. What, does 'the usual' mean something different on your planet, Stan? Jesus." I laugh, trying to keep the mood light, despite the orgasmic grunts eschewed from one of the TVs.

"Luke, you got the kid. You think it's such a great idea to drink a whole pint of whiskey and soda water?" he asks, giving me a very sincere look while scratching his hairy upper lip.

I feel the blood rush to my face in a flash of hot red steel. "Don't. Fucking. Tell. Me. How to raise my kid, Stan. Don't you fucking dare."

"How 'bout a light beer?" Stan asks, rubbing his cricket legs together pornographically.

As usual, that cricket noise fucks with my brain and I agree, "Yeah, give me a, um, Coors—no, Miller Light."

He acts accordingly and places a frothy pot of piss before my face. Thirsty, I decide I don't care and dive head-first into the toilet in front of me. Dirty amber everywhere. Formaldehyde and ammonia tickle the hair in my nose and at the back of my throat. When I pull out of the piss bucket, I'm rotten and yellow. Jaundiced the same way I was when I crawled out of my mother's womb.

"Wha's that?" the thing asks, pointing again.

"Politics, kid. I told ya." But then I notice he's pointing at the Giants game. "Oh, uh, that's baseball. You've watched some baseball before, right?"

"Ba—ba—baseball?" it says, fumbling with the missile-shaped Transformer. Focusing, I realize the kid's handling a dildo and, shocked, I quickly nab it from the kid and toss it behind the bar, giving Stan a dirty look as I do. I give him another look that says, "Filth. You breed nothing but filth." But he just flicks a few crusty bits from his mustache and smiles at me before returning to glass-washing duties.

"Yeah, ba-ba-baseball, dummy," I say, returning my attention to the pudgy parasite sitting next to me. "Jeez. It's like the greatest sport on the planet. Your ma never took you to a game? You mean to tell me you've been on this stinking planet for five years and she hasn't taken you to a Giants game?"

Big blue eyes look up at me and shake back and forth.

"Well, shit, you're in for some more real life experience, today, Tobster. I'm sure we can scalp tickets real cheap an inning or two or three in."

I down the bedpan of light beer, thank Stan, drop five dollars of Cameron's tip money on the bar, then grab the kid by the hand and yank him out of the bar into the hazy light of day.

"No! No! No!" I yell, seated in the upper deck behind the wall in left field. I grab Toby's little shoulders and push him back into his seat. All around us some people are trying to start the wave. "This is baseball," I tell him. "You don't do the wave. That's for those football fucks. Football—a game for complete fucking psychopaths, morons, and sheeple. No wave here, kid. You get me?"

Under a high sun and bright blue sky, he gives me a look like he doesn't get me at all. I'm used to that. Much, much older people give it to me all the time.

Behind us, the bay glistens while a succession of bloody horns and dorsal fins undulate in and out of it. The windsurfers, sailors, and kayakers pay it no mind. Every time a monster comes close to the shore, a wave of blood washes up and erodes the land a half-inch or so. Then the normal seawater crawls in and takes over. It shan't be long now, I think.

"Look," I say, grabbing him by the shoulders again and turning him toward me. "We're here to watch baseball. The *game*—that's what's important. Not waiting for some douchebag next to you to let you know it's okay for you to stand up and sit down again."

"Is fun," it says.

"Fun? *Fun*? What is it about baseball that you think it's supposed to be *fun*? Listen, kid, when you do the wave, you miss a pitch. You miss a pitch, you might miss anything—a fly-out, a ground out, a magnificent double play, a homerun, or the pitcher beaning the batter and then rushing the batter and digging his sharp pitcher-teeth into the batter's neck and drinking his blood before eating all the meat off his bones. You get me?" I ask, looking at the kid in a way that makes him understand I'm as serious as shit.

"Yeah," he says, smiling through his watery eyes. That makes me smile and I muss the kid's hair.

"It's just something my dad or my uncle or some homeless guy taught me a long time ago—you respect the game. See? It's better to watch the game and respect it than to fuck around like a clown and pretend the game doesn't matter. Because it matters, kid. Every second of it. Every crack of the bat. Every smack of the glove. Every black eye and ruptured tendon. Every concussion. Every brawl. Every pitch. It all matters. It all makes a world of difference. Every time you miss something, you are less a person than you were before. You're more dead inside. You're sick and rotting and bait on a hook. You're more like everyone around you. And this is baseball. This is *baseball*. It's our lives on the line, son. Everyone's."

"I know. I know now," he says, smiling and trying to hold my hand. I push his little paw away and give him a look that says, "*If* you try that again," so he stops and turns his attention back to the game like a good kid.

"Look, you watch our seats. I'm going to get a beer. You want one?" He looks at me with some stupid big-eyed look. "Fine, but don't complain when the seventh inning stretch happens and they're no longer serving."

"Listen, I knew all along you wanted ice cream. Another life lesson, though, son—you don't always get what you want."

"But, I want'ed ice keem, and I'm getting it," it says behind a green mint-and-chip-smothered smile. We're at an ice cream parlor on Embarcadero down the street from the ballpark.

"Well, yeah," I guffaw. "You're a kid. You're going to get a lot of the things you want. Just not always. When I was a kid, I got everything I wanted. My family took cruises for vacation. You know what cruises are?" I ask while scooping sloppy mouthfuls of rocky road into my face. It shakes its head no. "I'll tell you, then. You get on a big boat that's like a gigantic Las Vegas strip mall and you see the world—mostly third-world countries with beautiful coastlines. But you don't get off. You look at that world from a distance and jerk off. I've done it hundreds of times. It's what privileged folk do."

"Why?" he asks in between mouthfuls. He's already downed three scoops, but I figure, what's the point of having kids if you don't spoil them.

"'Why' is the most useless question," I say. "What do you want to do next, son?" I ask, using my spoon to scrape the last marshmallow and bit of chocolate ice cream from my oversized bowl. When I clear that part clean of rocky road a phrase appears in the bottom of the bowl: ENJOY ME.

"Now how did you get this little cutie in here," Syd asks, kneeling down and pinching the potato-head's cheek.

"I… uh… is he not *allowed* in here?" I ask, watching Astrid slide up and down one of the three silver poles on stage, her legs lean, long, and strong. Tubes of blue neon line the stage, and the black floor is full of sparkles like stars. Tables surround the stage and galactic floor, occupied by shadows of people. Overhead, Nine Inch Nails' "Hurt" plays and everyone's crying while fumbling with their belts and zippers and the waistbands of their tidy whities.

We're at Tassels 'N' Tipples in North Beach. Somewhere down the street and around the corner, Lawrence Ferlinghetti is burning incense, praying to Ganesha, and wishing he was me.

"Look, Luke, I know you're the… unconventional type, but, yeah, I'd say bringing a five-year-old to a strip club is not allowed," Syd says, standing up from Toby and looking me in the eye.

"Age is just a number," I say, unable to take my eyes off of Astrid. Astro Glide, her twin, soon joins her and straddles one of the other poles. Their blood-red hair flies and flails like flames as they shake their manes to the music and wiggle their hips to the melancholic strum of chords. The stage catches fire. My face heats up. The blaze illuminates the room and sickens me as I have to see everyone's faces, eyes, and how they bend in half so easily to mouth their own cocks while still watching the show, crying and scared. I freak for a second, but San Francisco's finest toss nickels and dimes at Astrid and Astro Glide, which stick in their soft, pale flesh, making them bleed profusely. Their blood douses the flames.

"I didn't realize there were so many cops in here," I say, removing my gaze from the stoning.

"That lady looks like mommy before she take a baths," Toby says, pointing at Astro Glide.

"No, kid. No, she really doesn't," I say. "Trust me."

"Seriously, Luke, you have to get him out of here. What were you thinking?" Syd asks, pulling her silk robe tighter around herself before reaching up to straighten her black-rimmed glasses. She's a student and only dancing to put herself through college at UC Berkeley. We connected months ago when she told me she loved Vonnegut, Milton, and Danielle Steel after a lap dance that left me somewhat messy but interested in her life story. Ever since, I've been compelled to aid her in her academic endeavors.

"I'm just trying to be a responsible father," I say, gazing at my own reflection in Syd's glasses, lost. "I'm just trying… I just…." I feel a lump in my throat and stop talking, fearing I might start crying. "I miss… I miss Cameron, Syd. I just miss her so much."

Then, like wet cardboard, I crumple into Syd's arms, sobbing like a five-year-old, leaving wet snotty marks all over her shoulder and chest. She holds onto me for a few seconds, patting my back with real warmth and affection before pushing me away and calling for the cops.

"There's no empathy in the world, Toby," I say, slinging him up over my shoulder while wiping my nose and eyes with my forearm and running for a big, blinding white rectangle of light that has the word "EXIT" blinking in red above it.

On John F. Kennedy Drive in Golden Gate Park I hand the kid his first piece. It's a SIG Pro semi-automatic. Atop a grassy knoll, we nestle in nicely behind a few large oaks and watch the cavalcade of cars parade down the street. I know the kid won't hit the broadside of a barn, so I'm not too worried. But, like a proud papa, I'm eager to see what he's capable of.

"It's just like *G.I. Joe*," I say, adjusting the handgun in his grip so that he's holding it right.

"G.I. Joe?" he asks.

"Oh, you're fucking kidding me. Kids these days. You really don't have any guidance."

An ocean breeze weaves over the treetops and loosens pine needles, leaves, and dreadlock-flakes into the air all around us like we're in one of those San Francisco snow globes they sell at Fisherman's Wharf.

After a time, I get through to the little potato-head. He grips the gun like he means it and seems excited about the possibilities. Of course, I have to help him hold the gun when he fires, otherwise he might hurt himself. As a sensitive member of the human race, I conscientiously make every effort to keep others from hurting themselves. No one should ever be responsible for their own pain. It's my solemn oath.

Since it's a game, we're waiting for a convertible. When one finally arrives all of 10 minutes later, I help the kid aim and squeeze the trigger—that's the key, I tell him, you *squeeze* the trigger, you don't pull it or yank it or get rough with it. You *pull* it. Treat it like a lady, I tell him. I figure I should get a couple life lessons wrapped into one with this one.

"Just pull the trigger," I say, my hand around his, pulling the trigger.

"I know," he says before the pop of the little gun bounces off the nearby trees and rattles the kid to the bone. But he doesn't cry. Such a good kid. Instead, he immediately registers the hole it made in the side of the Nissan Infiniti convertible. Better than that, he laughs. He laughs again when the Nissan Infiniti convertible fishtails and slams into a large oak across the street. That makes a much louder bang than the gun had. Though they weren't going that fast before we shot the car, the driver's head whiplashes hard into the steering wheel. The driver's door swings open after that and a man in a polo shirt and khakis falls out. His expensive hair piece askew atop his bloody scalp. On all fours, the man starts convulsing and vomiting into the green grass while people on the sidewalk pass him by and tell him to get a job and clean up his act. A tall blond exits the passenger side, makes her way behind the car and calls out for help while feeling at the blood trickling from her forehead. More people pass them and scorn them and spit and seem really disgusted.

"I think you've seen enough," I say, and grab the gun from the kid. We stand up from the dirt and pine needles and walk through the trees away from the sickening scene.

"Are you going to be my new dada?" Toby asks as I lift him onto the pink and purple horse of the merry-go-round. We're still in Golden Gate Park, just down the way from target practice.

"Well, guy, I don't know," I say. "Perhaps. I like your ma a whole lot. More than I've ever liked anybody."

"Back up, fella, we got to run this thing, you know," the merry-go-round operator yells at me. I shoot him a look that makes him back away and shut the fuck up.

"I tell momma that. I want a dada," the little shit says.

"You can just call me dad for now, okay?" I say.

"Okay, dada," he says, grinning like an idiot.

"I said you could call me *dad*," I say.

"Okay, da—dad," he says, taking hold of the plastic horse's reins.

"There ya go," I say. I muss his hair and step back from

the ride that glitters like marzipan cake. The weirdly shiny horses, with kids straddling them, starts to go 'round and 'round. Toby passes once, then twice, then a third time. Each time he waves and smiles. On the fourth, he blows a kiss and I make a mental note to remind him never to do anything like that again. The merry-go-round, as well as its calliope music, speeds up just then. Around and around they go. Way too fast. It's like something out of a cheesy Stephen King movie. The kids are screaming, the plastic horses are grinning wide and viciously. The music just keeps getting faster and faster. Comical, even.

When it doesn't slow down, but just keeps going faster and faster, I feel a little pulse of concern. Toby's passing by every two seconds, reaching out to me with a tear-stained and strained face. At the controls, the operator seems catatonic. He's leaning back away from the control panel, nibbling incessantly on his right thumbnail while his eyes stare straight forward and register nothing.

"Jesus! Are you doing anything about this?" I ask, stepping to the guy who seems shaken from his slumber. He leisurely turns knobs and pulls levers for show. "You're scaring the shit out of the kids!"

He fires a horse-toothed smile at me. "Shouldn't they be scared?" he asks.

"What the *fuck* are you *talking* about?" I ask, stepping closer to him.

"If they're going to grow up with people like you around,

shouldn't they be scared?" His grin gets even wider. He turns another knob and the merry-go-round spins even faster. "Hell, with people like me around they should be scared. But, you—you're a real piece of work. Let's let these kids know what they're in for." He turns another knob and the screams from the merry-go-round's strained mechanisms are masked only by the high-pitched screams of the kids on it.

I pounce on him. I push his surprisingly soft skull into the soft, grassy earth below him, and pummel it. I punch. I pound. I dig fingers into eyes and jam elbows into cheekbones and jaw. I yell, "You leave my kid alone!" and try to rip a rib from him with my bare fingers. When I realize I can't do that, and that the guy's unconscious, I give up.

Not really knowing how to run a merry-go-round, I fiddle with the controls until I see results. The swirl of cake-sweet colors the likes of puce, purple, cherry, and tonsils swirls to a slower revolution. A crunching sound of metal then echoes off the surrounding park trees, and the ride comes to a jarring stop, sending kids flying from their plastic horses into the golden bars they were just holding onto for support. Some go soaring and clunk into the metal floor of the carousel. Other little shits dart from their steeds and land teeth-first in the grass around the ride, squealing from their newly toothless and red-rimmed mouths as they call for their mommas. Those that are paying attention rush to their children and wrap them in their arms. I see that Toby's one of the few that managed to hold on and stay on his horse.

He's crying but seems unhurt and okay. Just scared and confused. He's looking all around at the kids with broken legs and arms and teeth, holding on tight and trying to breathe through his sobs.

I run to Toby and tell him it's going to be alright. I push through other parents tumbling through my path and pull him off the horse and tell him it's just a ride. It's just a merry-go-round. Just some stupid ride in the park. I tell him I'm here. I'm here for him. Cries and screams and wails siren around us in the bright tree-shadowed daylight. While patting his moppy hair back and wiping the tears and snot from his face, I tell him it's okay. I'm here. The ride's over. I'm here. I tell him there's nothing to fear. I tell him again, there's nothing, *nothing* to fear, even though I've never been more scared in my life.

QUAKING

Yesterday these sidewalks were blanketed with fallen leaves that rustled under my feet like the whispers of trampled, half-conscious children. Today, the wind that passes through my hangover head has shooed them all away. The only proof they were ever here at all lay in wet, leaf-shaped imprints in the concrete, which make the sidewalks look like star charts.

On my way to work, humping these steep hills of Leavenworth toward Aquatic Park where I work as an unlikely accountant for a commercial art gallery, I bend down to inspect a star-like shape in the walkway and nearly lose my balance. I watch my disappointing body roll down the sharp hill. Its head cracks open on the curb down there across the water from Alcatraz as my blood vacates my chicken-egg skull like so much yolk while also loosing that rat that crawled in there the other night and died before being shocked back to life when I rubbed my feet on the shag rug in Cameron's apartment above Bourbon Bandits. It crafted the circuit for life-giving electricity when I touched her cardigan-covered shoulder, unleashing a shockwave through each of our bodies. When it happened I thought that contact, that little spark could send us both back in time to a place where I could be a better person, someone capable of romance, big ideas, true responsibility and direction—a future. But as the electric crackle faded, she moved away, laughing and rubbing her shoulder saying "*Fuck*, Luke! Don't *do* that!" drawing out that last word like the end to a sad song.

Then her kid came running out of his room into hers, toe-headed and stupid and as small and filthy as a potato freshly ripped from the earth's damp soil, asking "What's *wong*, momma? What's wong?" and Cameron, faking a laugh, picked him up immediately, his fat, stubby arms quickly wrapping around her. With his doughy face turned toward me, he looked through me and pointed, kept pointing, confusing me as to what the fuck he was pointing at so I looked around and put my Winston out into my Lagunitas then hid my beer underneath the bed. Confused as to what else to do, I stuck my tongue out at the little shit but he kept pointing at me until Cameron saw me naked and told me to "Jesus! Put some fucking clothes on" while covering one of the kid's ears after throwing a blanket at me, then rocking the kid as though he couldn't have heard her filthy words through the ear she forgot to cover.

My whole body went red, having not realized I *was* naked, but the kid kept pointing and eventually said something that sounded like "fuck" but momma Cameron understood better and walked behind me, around the bed, and, with him in tow in the other arm, grabbed his toy truck and exited the bedroom. When I looked down I saw that I wasn't naked at all, dressed all the way up to my black tie and white shirt. I even had my shiny black shoes on. I rubbed them together to make a little song for myself and make myself feel just a bit better, which it did. So, I took out another Winston, got up and grabbed one more Lagunitas from Cameron's old, avocado-green refrigerator, popped it open and took a seat back on her bed with a sudden sense of overwhelming accomplishment.

Sitting there, I developed visions of *family*. Of something I wasn't sure I could ever know. Of Cameron, me, and her tiny, dirty, hair-topped potato taking trips to the park, the movies, the zoo, the aquarium. Of *us* buying the kid stuffed narwhals and ice cream cones and spending time together around the dinner table while the summer sun lingers outside, pushing a quiet yellow-brown light through the shades until the kid finally gets tired and hauled off to bed so Cameron and I can share time together, make each other our favorite drinks, laugh, flirt, play board games and listen to music as the light transforms into a warm moonlit glow that tells us to head off to bed, to make love quietly so as not to wake the kid, to fall asleep in each other's arms exhausted from the effort.

While immersed in these thoughts, sitting there at the end of Cameron's bed, my eyes inflated like blood-filled balloons and burst just before a new set of eyeballs rolled up from my guts, pushed their way through my constricting throat and popped back into the place of my old eyes. I wiped the bloody tears from my face, having sobbed so hard at the mere *idea* of happiness. Then, impatient, I stood at the doorway, exhaling smoke toward the kid's room until Cameron came back with the look of an exhausted trial on her face. I quickly retreated back to her bed, plopping down hard enough to make the bed shake and springs squeal, kicking my feet up with a smile that said: I'm happy here and not going anywhere.

"Seriously?" she said, nonelectric shoulders slumping.

"What?" I asked, cigarette smoke slipping from my mouth and the hole at the base of my skull where it meets the back of my neck.

"Luke, I told you to put on some fucking clothes," she said, arms folded, face stretched into seriousness.

"They burned," I told her, smiling.

"Luke! What the fuck are you talking about?" she asked, dropping her arms to her sides, still standing in the bedroom doorway, the hallway light haloing her slim figure.

"They burned. My clothes. *Myclothesmyclothesmyfamily*. Up in smoke… uh, just… just, um, my clothes," I trailed on, confused, not smiling, and wondering if I'd said too much.

"Luke, put some damn clothes on," she said, walking toward me and grabbing some other man's clothes from beside the bed and tossing them at me.

"These aren't mine, Cameron," I said.

"What are you talking about?" she asked, confused, but as her eyes settled on the pile she'd thrown at me, a look of alarm washed over her face.

I didn't want to hurt her feelings or start a fight because I wanted to stay, so, I put them on even though they were far too tight and obviously belonged to her Asian ex-boyfriend, Tam, that rode a Harley and played in a satanic death metal band called Hot Mayonnaise. I didn't even tell her that his clothes smelled like her pussy, though perhaps they smelled more like his. I couldn't remember.

After putting those clothes on, I leaned back on the bed again and felt another overwhelming sense of accomplishment. It was shaping up to be a great night. I believed Cameron and I were really going places.

Only then did I realize Cameron was already out of the clothes she had on earlier and was now in her bathrobe, smelling of cinnamon toothpaste and coconut lotion. She must have changed when she put the potato in his sack.

She clearly put the robe on in haste, however, and her breasts, though small, were almost falling out. Unable to control myself, I got hard. I smiled at her, told her she looked nice—that I liked her hair. Because the pants I wore were so constrictive, she noticed where I was going with that kind of saucy talk and responded by blowing a raspberry and giving me a thumbs-down.

Out her bedroom window, a sasquatch howled and

gutted a father of four on his way home from a 12-hour security guard shift at Walgreens. His pockets were full of the Altoids tins he'd pilfered on his way out, meant as a gift for the kids and payback to his employers for his lousy pay, but ended up as the perfect after-dinner compliment for his assailant. Various legs, arms, and heads also rolled up Geary Street in a flash flood followed by the acrid, thick perfume of bloody feces when the giant, tangled ball of intestines that daily patrols the entirety of San Francisco followed suit.

"Look, Luke," she told me. "I don't know what I was thinking asking you up here after work—"

"But you ask me up all the ti—"

"But clearly it was a mistake. I barely know you. I guess I just got lonely tonight and wanted some company—"

"But this isn't the first time I—"

"…and you were there, I guess. Just there. Like you always are at the end of almost all of my shifts at the bar—and even most of the beginnings of those shifts, now that I think about it. But, seriously, I really shouldn't be bringing people I don't know around my kid, you know? I hope you understand."

"Cameron, we've been sleeping together now for over…"

"I think you should go," Cameron said.

"I just want to be your dad."

"*What?*"

"I just want to be a father figure to the kid, if I can. Like, be a good influence and be there for him. If I can. And you, too—I want to be there for you, too, Cameron."

"Just, you know, go. Now. Please go." Her arms were crossed again, head down. She stepped out of the doorway so that I could see the front door more easily.

I felt hurt the way one is supposed to and my gut somersaulted. I pulled myself from the bed, touched her shoulder to see what would happen but nothing happened so I stumbled down the piss-wet stairs of her Tenderloin apartment building, tears streaming down my face, and skipped my way home up the hill around the corner, playing a game of hopscotch over decapitated bodies while smashing heads like rotten pumpkins against Union Square store fronts as soon as I found them trundling in the gutters, pulling themselves along by their tongues, licking at discarded cigarette butts, chewed gum, empty syringes, and used condoms. Whistling "Blue Skies" all the while.

I recall this bitter-sweetly in the fall morning light as I bend down to look at the leaf's imprint on the steep sidewalk hill of Leavenworth Street. I try to keep myself from crying, from wishing I had, in fact, cracked my head open just now so I could let it all out and be rid of it—but it's no good.

Everything—birds, trees, windows, parked cars, bones, and the candy wrappers in the gutters—rattles around me like gypsy music. My guts, my lungs, my heart, also shudder. My hands shake. They shake as I touch the imprint of the leaf, which really looks like a black star stuck in the sidewalk. My finger goes into it and there's nothing around my finger but the coldness of empty space—like a black star. I think about being born and my finger disappears within the leaf's imprint embedded in that grey concrete. I pull it out, confused. I think about having children of my own and I push it in again and the black star contracts, slowly closing up around my index finger, so I pull it out and look again.

It's just a leaf's imprint on the cold sidewalk.

I can't tell what I'm doing wrong.

When I try to touch the barren black starhole again it quivers and the wind moans my name and the trees call me sick and twisted while telling me to hurt them, to strangle them, to pull their limbs back and spank them. I quickly thrust my index finger in again and the whole sidewalk suddenly ripples into a wave that rolls all the way down the hill causing the asphalt to undulate and parked cars to hop like frogs, many of their windows shattering from the activity. From the force of my penetration, the black star puckers, flutters, and tightens around my finger, so, I decide to put my middle finger in there and attempt to loosen it up, slowly spreading my two fingers apart to pry it open. Those fingers go wet with blood and a sensuous cracking sound greets my ears. Then the wind wails and the blue bay about four blocks down the hill shimmies and glitters with hints of red leaking from its sore, raw edges like blood from pinpricks.

The sidewalk again swells and crests.

I hear "Jesus! Put some fucking clothes on" and th more moaning. Then, "Get out." Then, "No—more." So I put a third finger in and everything shudders more violently and there's electricity ringing up from my knuckles all the way to my elbow like when I touched Cameron's sweatered shoulder. And now Cameron's face contorts in front of me. It pulls up through the cement in the sidewalk, grey and cold and wanting me. A warm fluid makes its exodus and splashes across my midsection as her body splits in two down the middle like an axed piece of veiny firewood, arteries ripping, then suturing themselves back together beneath me while the trees' bare limbs rattle and their roots push hard up against the surface and the houses around me bow and breathe like wooden giants in the gale and I hear the sirens singing to me the way they've sung to me my whole life. Those sirens whip up their songs from the edges of the city but the sky isn't changing from its soft contrast of ash and blue as everything below it forcefully tries to change its shape, tries to metamorphosize into the monster it is. It all looks so normal as the monster, which is the city incarnate, forcefully tries to penetrate its dozen bloody horns and tendrils through the earth's crust while at the same time its scaly back arches out of the bay in an eruption of salt water and breaks the Golden Gate into a thousand shards before serpentining through the water to the Bay Bridge to collapse that, as well, ensuring what we all fear: That we're stuck here. It's not just a choice to never leave this place and visit the real world.

As my fingers, one after the other, become a fist and get lost inside the black star, I feel myself go hard. Now I'm on the sidewalk, pressing my face against the grey concrete, trying to get a closer look at this black star fallen into my path, the ground turbulent and waving as I whisper "What do you want?" and "Why me?" while I attempt to glimpse what's on the other side of time and reality as my fist slips inside the black imprint and the star wraps itself tightly, now, around my wrist without submission, crushing it, the bones splintering with the sound of large trees teetering and crashing against the street, against houses already crumbling as everything in my arm pops with finality. Lights flash behind my closed eyelids as the hole pulls me in further, squeezes, tugs and pulverizes my fist, my wrist, tendons and all, veins popping like garden hoses folded over themselves unable to handle the immense pressure of blood doing everything it takes to reach its unappreciative brain.

I try to push myself up away from the sidewalk. The pulsating black imprint of the leaf gapes open wide for a moment like a breathless mouth finally taking some oxygen, stretching open more than thought possible before it snaps back tight with lightning quickness, yanking me in so fast I smash my skull against the concrete and go out into the blackness of that absent night.

When I come to I'm in the back of an ambulance and sirens are everywhere and I want to tie myself to the ship's mast and be fed to them even though nothing in my body seems to be moving and there are two or three uniformed people over me mining my body for gold and saying things like "There's no use" and "We've done everything we can" and "What do you think we can get for this?" and the other says "Nothing" looking over a chunk of me, following that up with "fool's gold" and I'm yelling "Hit me with the defibrillator! Please! Hurry! Please! There's not much time left! Put a spark in me! Light me up!" and then the glimmer I thought I could see radiating out of me all my life starts to dim, dull, flicker, and finally go out like a city in a power outage.

And then they're trying to tell me what has happened to me, and I can't move or get out so I try to breathe through the waves of pain and morphine and not listen to them and instead tell them what actually happened. I say, "I saw the world open up for me and invite me in. It wanted me. It wanted to love *me*. Me! I'm telling you... you have to listen. When the world wants you, you listen. You *listen* and you don't fight it and you thank you're fucking lucky *stars*! You give it what it wants. It wanted *me*. It wanted my children. It wanted my seed. It wanted... it wanted us to be a *family*. Cameron, please, kiss it and put a Band-Aid on it," I say, yanking one of the EMT's heads down to my bloodied crotch, the ache and absence there turning now into a hot tingle under the song of sirens and the trundle of tires. But those people looming over me in fluorescent lamplight just pat my shoulder, push me back down on the gurney, tell me not to speak, and say "It's okay, fruitcake" and "Just try to calm down" and then they keep saying "Don't speak" and "It's okay" like I'm too stupid to know any better. And as I'm lying there I realize I cannot make a fist or hear my own breath or feel a heartbeat and eventually, after a long ride that doesn't end at the hospital or my home or Cameron's, I also notice no sparks of electricity are flying, not anywhere.

A PARADE, ALWAYS

The light's hazy the way I remember it from childhood. Always hazy. The way the light back then sifted through the Sacramento smog and caked the air over endless flat fields next to freeways and highways and beneath overpasses. That light seeps into the bar through big front windows as the sun sets out there, ready to plop into the ocean, fizzle, and send a tsunami of boiling water our way to free us from our skin and bones in a violent act of forgiveness. No artificial lights—expect the strings of holiday lights around the stage at the back—are on to interfere with this natural phenomenon I can only recall in my few memories of childhood. It gives me a giddy sense of innocence as I drink another glass of Jim Beam and blow smoke from my Winston into my friends' faces, smiling an ugly smile that turns beautiful in the sandpaper light.

Me, Sanchez, Kevin, and Russ sit around a round table at the Pelican's Bill in Oakland discussing rat bites and the best ways to treat them. The cure for the itch they make in the sores all over our bodies is our holy grail. We're also congratulating ourselves endlessly on what a great reading we just gave at some hole-in-the-wall around the corner, despite the fact that we were the only audience for it. I pitch Russ a quarter and tell him to go find our holy grail. He waddles over to the jukebox and plays The Fall's "Eat Y'Self Fitter".

As Sanchez and Kevin debate the merits of Sanchez's pencil mustache, a skinny kid in filthy jeans and denim jacket stumbles in, nearly falls down the two steps leading into the stage-room and tumbles into me, knocking me and Jim Beam from my chair. The back of my head clacks good with the cement floor. The kid, probably 20, rolls off of me, pushes himself from the floor, wipes his nose, twitches, looks down at me and smirks, twitches again, and turns to walk away.

"What the *fuck*?" I yell, feeling a bit dizzy from the hit as I stand up.

"Excuse me?" he asks, turning back toward me.

"Exactly, shithead. That's what you should be saying. Nobody in this whole goddamned state has an ounce of manners."

Without a second's thought, he walks over and slugs me in the jaw; however, its effect is almost comical as it lands with all the force of a large horsefly. I don't flinch or even stumble back a half step. It's like he slapped me with a helium balloon.

Instead, I feel the sun boil the ocean. I see all of

Cameron's dead babies bleeding out of it. I see the earth erode at its watery edges. I see the light. I see God in love and violence.

Shaking the illusion from my jostled skull, I grab the kid by his jean jacket and throw him across the table where Sanchez and Kevin sit. They're mildly amused as he fumbles to get himself off the table now slippery with whiskey, vodka, and the strips of skin that have been peeling off me all day.

When he manages himself away from the table, I grab him again, throw him against the wall, and put my fist through his skull, which collapses like a rotten pumpkin. He slinks down the wall into a sitting position, pumpkin-head to the left, shoulders slumped, veins of red mucus spilling from his jack-o-lantern mouth.

I regain my seat just as the middle-aged female bartender strolls over with extra-large breasts and sinewy arms, each of which make me flinch and quiver.

"We don't much care for people coming in here and beating up our regulars," she says. "That's Tommy. He wouldn't hurt a fly. Couldn't if he wanted. We like him. You better leave before I call the cops."

I look at Sanchez and Kevin, who suddenly don't know me anymore. They saunter away from the table and over to the bar, grab a stool and call Russ over to them and look every which way but at me directly.

When I exit the bar I pull my Winstons out of my pocket and find they've been turned to confetti. A young couple stands near me by the front windows of the bar smoking, so I ask them for a cigarette.

"Sure," the guy says.

I put the cigarette in my mouth and the girl cups a flame to my face and lights it.

"We never liked Tommy," she says. "We saw what you did in there. We've wanted to kick that fucking kid's face in for years now. But we're pacifists."

"That bartender said he's a regular. That people like him," I say, blowing smoke.

"That's horseshit," the guy says. "She's just a fucking sadist. That's her son. She knows he's a fuckup and a junky so she calls him down here knowing he'll do something stupid and by night's end get his face broken. It's her sick way of teaching the punk a lesson, I guess. I mean, look," he says, pointing toward the bar's windows.

Inside, she's leaning across the bar chatting gleefully with my friends, everyone laughing as she pours them shots while they, in unison, flip me off, and continue laughing.

I look down the street, past the nearly vacant downtown of Oakland filled with featureless buildings that give off the air of not having been frequented by a living being for centuries. Low grunts and sick coughs sound from the shadows. The orange nickel of the sun dips into the horizon's slot and is gone.

"You wanna come back to our place and get fucked up?" the girl asks.

"Sure," I say.

We're walking through alleyways between dumpsters and garage doors covered with graffiti. As we walk, those illicit illustrations make a movie, one after the other depicting me as a small child chewing on my fingers then my arms, blood coating my mouth until I'm armless. Then I start in on my legs. The last few frames are my pathetic, limbless attempt at eating my own torso, my child's mouth snapping like a Doberman's, teeth clicking with each attempt, blood and spit and snot flying from my crazed mouth and nose, accomplishing nothing.

"Here," the guy says, handing me a joint. I take a drag and immediately my feet turn to cinderblocks and my head goes fuzzy in the haze of sunset, the grey and rose-hued illumination of the air.

"Are we gonna fuck him?" I think I hear the girl say through the cloud weighing my head down. My feet make the sound of machinery flattening sheet metal with each step.

"Um? What? Huh?" I say, concentrating hard on walking a straight line as I hand the joint back.

"She said we're going to fuck you," he says, putting the joint to his lips and passing it off to his girlfriend.

"Um, no thanks," I say. "No. No thanks."

I stop and shake my legs, trying to expel the concrete in my veins that's hardening and petrifying my bones in the process.

"Actually, she said we're going to fuck you and tear you in two. Right down the middle," he says. "Then we're going to have two of you so we don't have to share. We'll keep half of you in the freezer, the other half in bed. We'll take turns or draw straws to see who gets the warm half."

He tells me this while they stand 10 feet in front of me, holding hands and taking long puffs on the joint. Their eyes stay fixed on me as the garage doors and dumpsters now show home movies of me as a child climbing trees in the front yard. Then I'm at school, 13-years-old, in the utility closet with Mrs. Hammerstein, my geometry teacher. Her mouth is wrapped around my cock, working vigorously at it, even though I came 10 minutes prior and only 30 seconds after she put her lips to it. The film jump-cuts to her decapitated head lying on the highway a few hours after the closet scene, her eyes open and staring, two cars behind her head married in a convulsive twist of metal. My sperm, which had caught in her sinuses, leaks out of her nose onto the asphalt.

When I look away from the picture show, the couple's no longer anywhere to be seen. My head goes even hazier than before. The light hangs about my peripherals, fuzzy. A kind of static in the air.

"Hey… hey!" I yell, feeling lost, feeling like I lost something—feeling that hollow presence of a just-missed opportunity.

Confused, I wander the alleys as the light refuses to fade, staying grey and grainy, its particles parting and sprinkling away where my hands penetrate it and push through it with swimming and fighting motions. In the wake of those actions, the particles all float back into their original places behind me.

Voices come from the dumpsters. Thousands of whispers all talking over one another so I can't tell what they want. And they refuse to stop until I finally look in a red dumpster and find a mountain of discarded tongues. Then I realize it's just a pile of tiny, hairless, baby rats, and they're asking me for a home. I tell them I'm sorry. That I don't even have a home of my own. That I can barely remember what home is.

Suddenly, I hear someone call my name. I look up from the dumpster to the upstairs window of a two-story house. It's opened just a crack. My name leaks out of it once more. The house doesn't look finished, its insulation exposed, the Spanish tiles on the roof in piles and not yet laid.

A blurry face passes quickly behind the glass of that second-story window. "Luke! Get the fuck up here! We've been waiting for you."

That's my home, I think. But I don't live here. But that's my home. But I don't have a home. But, I think that's my home. Who's in my home? Who the fuck is *invading* my home?

Angered, I push away from the dumpster, walk through the waist-high chain-link gate leading into my home's backyard. In it, there's a yellow and green swing set and an orange and black Big Wheels, and a dwarfed dogwood in the corner. When I was eight I buried a time capsule there in a small styrofoam cooler. Before I know it, my hands are ripping through the earth below the dogwood, tearing away root and dry soil until my knuckles scrape the cracked top of my childhood treasure chest. Excited, I pull it out, sit back with it between my legs and peel off the lid. I can hardly contain my enthusiasm at finding what I had left for myself 23 years ago.

"Luke, goddammit!" I hear from the window above.

But I ignore it, salivating. First, I pull out Mark McGwire's 1984 US Olympics baseball card. I place it carefully beside me on the dying grass of the backyard lawn. Next, I discover a clear cassette tape, a forgotten relic. It's RUN D.M.C.'s album, *Raising Hell*. It's a tape that got me 40 lashings with a ruler the day I brought it to St. Patrick's Elementary and played it for my friends, two at a time, as we listened through the clunky headphones of my Sony Walkman.

Following that, there's a picture of my girlfriend from the third grade, Jenny. It's her school photo. She was embarrassed by her new braces, so, her smile looks forced and scared. I remember telling her to take pride in her metal, that she could probably pick up radio signals now and maybe even hear Martians. Soon after, she said she didn't want to be my girlfriend anymore.

I place her photo next to Mark McGwire's baseball card. Then I unfold a newspaper, the front page displays a large photo of billowing, worming white clouds twisting across an azure sky where the Space Shuttle Challenger blew up. I was eight-years-old when that happened and it was the first time I cried about something happening to people who weren't in the Bible.

After that, I find a model airplane of the Enola Gay wrapped in less remarkable newspaper. I make airplane sounds, weaving it through the air before my face, flying it over the recently excavated contents of my time capsule, making sounds of repetitive bombings. Next, I remove some baby teeth and shake them in my fist like dice before pulling out my first rosary and a gold crucifix that the silver body of Christ had broken off from. I search for Jesus in the Styrofoam cooler, but apparently he'd risen yet again. I rub the cold bones of my baby teeth in my palm and think how strange it is that they're still on this planet, and that I can confirm that, whereas the 50-cents that they earned me cannot be—that 50-cents that I got from having little bones in my young jaw torn out via string and door handle.

I then grab some old toys from the dirt-covered styrofoam box—action figures of Boba Fett, Zartan, Tron, Andre the Giant, and an angry hamburger that eats people instead of the other way around. Finally, at the bottom, there's a medium-sized velvet jewelry box. I pry it open to find my mother's shriveled, mummified heart. It looks more like the nub of a dried up tongue, or baby rat, maybe, but I know it's the heart because it's still beating a little.

Satisfied, I clump everything together, drop it back into the cooler, and rebury it. A plaintive cry from the window behind and above me rings out, "Luke!"

"Okay, already! I'm coming!"

I pull myself from the dusty lawn, brush myself off and walk up the concrete walkway along the side of the unfinished house to the door where I push into the garage and nearly crash into the orange 1974 Mazda 808—the compact car my mom drove through most of the 80s. I remember being driven home from school once and getting car sick. I quickly rolled the window down, stuck my head out, and let my vomit fly out the speeding vehicle where it landed with a flat smack against the following car's windshield. My mom said I was a good boy and my older sister and little brother giggled wildly. But my mom said I was a good boy so I didn't care about their mockery.

My BMX bike hangs from the rafters that I once rode around the block 107 times before telling my mom, proud of the accomplishment. An oil painting my dad did of Jesus on a green hill next to a lemon yellow sun leans against some shelves. He could have made millions from it if he'd sold it because it captured something most religious art didn't in a very direct way—sometimes you look at it and Jesus is there, other times he's not. My mother never liked it, however, and threw it out before those millions could be realized.

Inside the house, I find no familiar surroundings and my feet again feel like cinderblocks. I hear my name once more but can't tell now where it's coming from. The kitchen I'm standing in has a concrete floor, the counters and cupboards are just shells of their future selves. The whole house is incomplete.

I pass through the living room and the den and find the

stairs. Hazy light filters through the dust my feet kick up on the bare wooden steps. An open space comprises the top floor, all white. The floor, white. The walls, white. The ceiling, white. Clean and uncluttered. There is one space in this open expanse, though, sectioned into a little walled-off room in the corner. The door's open. "Luke," weakly issues from it, followed by gurgling.

Looking into the small walled-off room, I spot a naked couple propped up against the mirrored doors of the closet, their limbs entangled and heads drooping, their skin a sickly green. It's the couple from the alleyway, though they must be at least 20 years older now. It seems neither is breathing. I lean down, put my hand to the woman's cold breast and feel no heartbeat. When I remove my hand a cloud of dust and gnats envelopes my face and I cough and cough until I find myself out of the room and standing in the open expanse of the floor sticking my head out the window and yelling my own name in between coughs. During the coughing fit I watch my 12-year-old self down in the backyard digging. Then he's gone and it's just dying grass in grey, grainy light.

Behind me, the room's door closes with a clack. Wet skin slaps together, and someone grunts in response to a repetitive thud. When I open the door the man I thought was dead forcefully rams his cock into the woman's ass that I thought was also dead. While he pounds her ass, she's also astride a man with long hair I hadn't noticed in the room prior, his cock in her pussy. After a few dramatic moans, she slides away from both of them. The man on the bottom now fingers the vagina located just below his shrunken, tiny ball sack. The woman takes his small, finger-like penis in her mouth, slurps and moans.

They finally notice me spying after a few minutes. The couple I thought I knew yells in unison, "Jesus, Luke! Get out!" Then they throw a nearby pillow and say it again. Bewildered, I duck the thrown pillow, close the door, and walk back to the window overlooking the backyard where I yell my own name again until I see myself swinging on the yellow and green swing set. My younger self stops swinging, slaps his arm, then pulls the mosquito from it, its blood pocket now squished and empty, the blood only a small red splotch on his arm. He then puts the mosquito in his mouth and swallows, which causes me to yell out "Luke, goddammit!" yet again as he disappears.

A ripping roar unrolls behind me from the closed-off room, eschewing forth from what I can only imagine to be a chainsaw. Someone's in there growling and barking, as if scared of the chainsaw. A man's voice yells, "Good doggy. Yeah, there's a good little bitch," and then the whole floor shakes as something big and heavy drops. A woman's blood-curdling scream cries out, and I rush to the room, worried for the girl who promised me so much love earlier in the day. Reopening the door, I find a room full of hanging, formless, swaying meat, and a man in a burlap mask cutting through it all. The woman I heard scream lies on the floor beneath it all, the meat dropping all around her as she fingers herself and screams in ecstatic agony, the floor glazed with blood. A headless hermaphrodite is crumpled behind her, his head nowhere to be found in the room of cut up meat.

Again, annoyed, the two yell at me to get out.

A few moments later they exit the room, covered in blood and animal byproducts. "Luke, man," the guy says. "You really should call before coming over. At least knock, for fuck's sake."

"Knock?" I ask.

"Yeah, man."

"Knock? You killed someone in there. You were hurting *her*," I say, pointing to the woman sweeping sheets of blood from the insides of her thighs.

"Christ's sake, Luke, we were filming a porn. Don't get all bent out of shape. You know this is what we do. And you nearly fucked up the shooting," she says.

"A porn? What about the headless person in that room?" I ask.

"Headless? Luke, man, that's a RealDoll. A movie prop. It's not a person," he says.

"And, honey, it's just porn," she says. "Just a porn. We've been filming all day. Ever since you woke this morning."

"No, I… saw it move. Saw it breathe, touching itself."

"It's a pretty realistic doll, Luke," she says.

Unconvinced, I run back into the room. Chunks of meat swing from the ceiling and cover the floor, though the headless body of the hermaphrodite is absent. I get on my hands and knees and brush through the pooled, coagulating blood, moving aside bits of this and that, looking for anything I can identify as human, but finding nothing I recognize.

My reflection in the mirrored closet doors casts me naked and covered in a brown slick of oxygenating blood, surrounded by anonymous masses of meat. But I don't even remember getting out of my clothes. This is a scene I do recognize.

Flinging open the mirrored closet doors makes my blood-soaked visage disappear. Inside the walk-in closet, shelves of decapitated heads stare me down. I'm sure I recognize the head of the long-haired person from their earlier filming, just as I'm sure that Mrs. Hammerstein's head also sits among their collection. There must be a couple dozen heads here, if not more.

A hand firmly takes hold of my shoulder, and I'm reassured by the contact.

"Fake, Luke. All fake," he says.

"They don't look fake," I say before falling to my knees and puking, yelling out my own name over and over with each convulsion.

The self-proclaimed porn stars grab me under my armpits and haul me naked from the room and sit me in front of the window overlooking the backyard.

"Just calm down, Luke. It's not like you haven't seen this before," the guy says while tying on a butcher's apron. Then he turns and stomps back to the room.

While I'm trying to figure out how the light has yet to fade into night, I feel a pleasant sensation and look down through my stupor to find the woman's mouth spread around my cock, bobbing up and down with a brutal force. I come almost immediately but she doesn't stop, working her tongue and mouth around my increasingly limp dick. I don't want her to get mad at me, so I don't tell her to stop. I sense the frustration in her jaw muscles, however, and her teeth slowly sink into the base of my cock, so I finally push her off me. She falls back, wipes her mouth, and laughs.

"Baby, baby, baby," she says. "What's the matter, my baby? I just wanna play teacher and student, baby. Let's play."

"I don't want to," I say, and I really don't, but I feel tempted anyway and find it hard to resist.

"Let's play, motherfucker. Let's play, you piece of shit. You're my toy. You're my *thing*. You're mine. You understand? You do what I fucking say, little boy. You hear me? Now put that throbbing cock in momma's ass."

"No!" I yell. "No, no, no! I don't wanna! I don't wanna! You can't make me!"

"Shit, calm down. I'm just playing. It's just a porn, Luke, like I said. Look, I'll even turn the cameras off," she says, picking up a tiny remote from beside her on the floor. She points it at the corners of the room and for the first time I see the white surveillance cameras stationed there.

The chainsaw growls again in the other room.

My clothes, they're in the far corner. Standing, I rush for them and the woman lunges at me, missing awkwardly, slamming her head against the floor, and knocking herself out. My pearly sperm drips from her mouth onto the white floor. That chainsaw roars and chews through more flesh and bone in the other room, so I grab my clothes in a bundle and hustle down the stairs, out through the garage, and into the backyard where I slip into my pants, shirt, and shoes in a huff.

Traipsing into the alleyways I follow a maze of dumpster-lined corridors in a hazy, speckled light that hasn't changed since just before sunset. In a half-run, I spill out of the alleys onto a main thoroughfare of Oakland just as the sun comes up, basking this wasteland in a clear, ultraviolet white light.

Standing in the middle of the street, I'm surrounded by large animals floating and bobbing in the sky. There's a black and white cat, a yellow dog, and a blue and red woodpecker. Marching bands stomp past me blowing their trumpets and crashing their cymbals. The mayor rolls past in the back of a flatbed truck, waving to and fro and blowing me a kiss. Then the Oakland A's high-step through, poking each other in the ass with hypodermic needles, followed by floats representing the varied cultures of the Bay Area—everything from Vietnamese and Irish to Russian, Japanese, Polish, and zombie. That's followed by floats for local banks, tax collectors, and universities, each made out of butchered meat. Then it's all clowns, baton-throwers, fire-eaters, and contortionists crab-walking down the street toward the boiling water of the bay.

I drop down to the asphalt on my hands and knees, gigantic balloons blocking out the sky as feet kick and stomp past every side of me. I vomit over and over again and hyperventilate, choking on sobs as high school gymnasts and county fair beauty queens twirl by me.

It's a parade, I think. It's a parade. It's just a parade, I tell myself.

MUMMY

I'm at my apartment building on Leavenworth and Post. It's midnight and a new day and I'm drunk, a little bit high, hungry, tired, and bathed in white moonlight and stripper-sweat from an earlier visit with Syd where she remained fully clothed and expressed her views, passionately, on the current White House administration and how its theme of perceived isolation is mirrored in Ballard's *Concrete Island.* Fumbling with my keys at the building door, they drop to the concrete and shatter like glass in a kind of beautiful way, sparking into nothingness at my feet. I try the door and find it is indeed locked, so I ring the building manager's apartment. He doesn't answer for four or five or more buzzes, until he finally does.

"You know what time it is?" the voice asks, groggy and gravelly. I know little about him except that he's probably 10 or 15 years older than me and he's your typical San Francisco pothead—filthy and lazy and pretty boring, but mostly unobtrusive, at least.

"Yeah, *Moonbeam*, shit—I know how to read a clock, goddammit—digital or not. I got my edjumacation, did you? Or did your soft little skull take one too many poundings inside your ma's womb while she was getting gangbanged by the Hells Angels in the fucking free-loving 60s? Anyway, I lost my keys. Can you just let me in?" As I'm leaning down, talking into the intercom, which is covered in some mysterious, viscous grey film, I realize I'm scratching at my left hand and lengths of skin are peeling away.

"Who is this?" he asks through the crackling, muffled intercom.

"It's Luke, man. Come on, just buzz me in," I say, still scratching away at my left hand, strips of dry skin curling up like pink crepe paper and falling to the concrete.

"Luke?"

"Yeah. Jesus, it's Luke. Let me in. I'm hungry and I'm tired and I just want back in my cell, Rainbow Meadows. Open up, compadre. Exprechen eee doytch?"

"Luke? Luke who, man? There's no Luke in the building, man," Sir Flower Power says, and I can tell he's just about to drift back into his weed-induced coma.

"Enough fucking around," I say, no longer finding anything funny. "It's Luke. I'm in motherfucking 4G. Luke, motherfucker. Wake up out of your skunk-junked haze and let me the fuck in! I just want to go home. Let me in. *Now*."

"Sorry, my friend—"

"We're *not* friends!" I yell.

"...but you're going to have to sleep this off somewhere else."

"What the fuck are you talking about, *Charles*? Jesus. Let me in! Quit fooling around!"

"You don't live here, man. The park's a good place to sleep. Go catch some Z's under the stars, man. You'll figure out where you should actually be after you sleep this one off. You might even learn something about yourself. Best of luck to ya, buddy."

"Charles? Charles!" I yell, but he doesn't respond so I buzz his apartment a hundred times and get no response, completely freaking out every time I have to touch the button on the intercom covered with this quivering grey film.

By the time I pull my left hand away from the intercom all the skin's gone from it. It's just muscle, sinew, and bone, and it glistens in the moonlight and smarts with every mild breeze.

"Fuck!" I yell and kick the door and back away into the street, which is mostly free of cars but for a few lurking taxis and foot-dragging zombies. The traffic lights at the intersection click from green to yellow to red, anyway, putting a halt to ghosts on their ways home.

My phone's in my left pants-pocket and when I reach for it I howl out in surprised pain, forgetting the state of my hand, so, I awkwardly reach across myself with my right hand and dig the phone out and call Kevin. It rings only a few times before he answers, as he's probably up talking to Christy and smoking a million cigarettes and telling her fascinating stories about one of the times he fashioned a perfect heart atop a perfectly crafted cappuccino.

"Hey, Kevin, it's Luke. I'm locked out of my apartment."

"Luke? Um, dude, just buzz your building manager to let you in. Why are you calling me?"

"Listen, genius, I already did that. Don't you think I already thought to do that? *Fuck*! That hippie fuck couldn't remove himself from his everlasting pot-smoke cloud long enough to meet me back in reality," I say, now scratching at my right hand, which holds the phone to my ear. "Come on, I need a place to crash while Prince Charles of the Poppy Fields sleeps off his stupid drug-induced life."

"Um, *Luke*, is it? Luke, I really don't know who the fuck you are—"

"Don't even *start* with the funny guy routine, Kevin—"

"...but I don't know how you got this number and I don't know why you're calling me this late at night and—" I hear Christy laughing in the background, telling him to just hang up on the *fucker* and come back to bed.

"Kevin! Come on! I just need a place to crash. I just need a place to crash, man. Let me come over and I promise I won't make a scene or get in your way with Christy. I'm cool with that. I'm *cool* with that, you understand me? Whatever. I don't even fucking care right now that you totally stole her away from me. I really don't care!"

"I'm hanging up now," Kevin says, and he does and I'm holding back the urge to riot and burn down this whole fucking city by myself.

Instead, I walk a few blocks down the city hill, deeper into the Tenderloin where Sanchez lives, and ring him up on my phone. I'm standing in front of his building on O'Farrell and Leavenworth. It's a dull pink building and the cockroach-infested sandwich shop he lives above has had its windows broken out. His window a few stories up is dark but lights up after the first couple rings.

"Sanchez, it's Luke. I'm locked out of my apartment. Can I crash on your floor just for the night?"

"Luke?" he asks.

"Yeah, it's me, man. Sorry. Shit. I know it's late. But fuck, just let me up. I need a place to crash."

"What the fuck is wrong with your hands?" he asks, and when I look up at his window I see Sanchez standing there in his wife-beater and pajama pants.

"Never mind about my fucking hands. Can I crash here?"

"Seriously. Are you wearing Halloween skeleton gloves? Are those hip again? When did those get hip again?" he asks as his voice drifts off into thought, finishing with "I wonder where I can get a pair at this time of year," which is barely audible.

"Earth to Sanchez! Can you ever think about anything other than fashion and your fucking pencil 'stache? Just let me come up!"

"You said your name was Luke, right? What, did I meet you at a party or something? Maybe a reading? Look, if I gave you my number then, or at any other time, I wasn't hitting on you. Lots of people seem to confuse that. And I'm not gay, so—"

"Don't fuck with me, Sanchez! This is not fucking funny!"

"I'm sorry if I gave you the wrong impression. I shouldn't have given you my number in the first place, let alone my address. Not that I remember doing either. Look, whatever your name is, go sleep it off elsewhere. I'm sure there's some other minor literary celeb willing to let you suck them off for a warm place to sleep. Maybe give Ferlinghetti a buzz."

His square of yellow flickers dark.

"Sanchez!" I scream, absolutely fucking livid at this bullshit prank my friends seem to be pulling. All the while I'm scratching at my arms, skin flaking off like chunks of bark now. Every gentle little breeze weighted down with the scent of piss stings like a bitch and it's all I can do to keep from gnashing my teeth to dust, biting back the pain.

With heavy, angry steps, I march on toward Russ's apartment on Turk and Larkin, sheets of skin shaken away from me with each footfall. His place is above Harry's Pub, and when I arrive I spot him standing outside the bar's door, smoking a cigarette and kind of hunkering down to talk to Bob, this midget stage-actor that lives in the neighborhood who's known for his operatic singing voice and ability to take on any role in any Shakespeare play at the drop of a hat. Despite his talents, he has to slum it like the rest of us in this shithole.

"Russ, thank fucking Christ," I say, interrupting their conversation. They both look at me with annoyed, disgusted expressions and take quick, nervous drags from their cigarettes. Russ, who's well over six-feet and 250-pounds, turns his back to me, completely blocking me off, and continues his high-energy chat with Bob.

"Russ… Russ… Russ… Russ…" I say, scratching my face while facing his back which you could easily project a major motion picture onto.

With a snotty little sigh and guffaw, Russ finally turns toward me and says, "Man, you fucking reek. I don't mean to be rude, but it's true. Just, you know, go take a bath. And, if you don't mind, I'm trying to have a conversation with my friend here. So, please, just leave us alone."

"Russ, don't fuck with me. I get it. You're all playing a joke on me. You, Kevin, Sanchez—even my fucking building manager," I say, suddenly feeling a little less conviction in the statement. I scratch at my face and feel something hang and dangle from my cheekbone. It flaps in the wind and distracts me so I pull at it and peel it away, dropping a flap of flesh to the sidewalk. They both look at me, repulsed, and start to walk away.

"Russ, come on, man," I say, following just behind them, scratching at my face, neck, arms, crotch. But they pick up their pace and when they turn the corner I turn with them and they pick up the pace even more and, finally, when Bob's little legs can't keep pace with Russ's giant strides, Russ picks him up and cradles him in his arms and gallops into a full-on sprint away from me toward Market Street and the oversized moon now hanging in that direction. They cross Market just before a streetcar can trundle over them.

I yell Russ's name one last time and give up, seeing they're no longer there after the MUNI passes, and decide to retreat back to Harry's Pub. It's a small, dank, urine-fouled place and when I walk in I feel right at home. At the bar a few of my teeth fall out as I attempt to get the bartender's attention. Then I see myself in the mirror behind the bar: sores all over my face and neck, my lips blackened, chapped, and broken, and the cheekbone under my left eye completely exposed. And my skinned hands, of course, which have gone numb now and are no longer hurting. Alarmed, however, I am not. I know far too well that this is life, and all things come to pass.

The lady bartender here at Harry's has a doughy figure with a face of crusty powder and makeup and she's losing her hair and wearing a top with a low neck that nearly lets one of her droopy breasts fall out. I catch just a hint of a pancake-sized nipple and look away.

"What can I get ya, sweetheart?" she asks and I tell her a

Jim Beam and she says great and tells me I have a beautiful smile and when I notice she's also missing a few teeth I tell her the same. She thanks me, takes the last of the money I have left in this world, and says it's real good to see me, that it's been a while, and though I don't recall ever being in Harry's Pub, I tell her "ditto" then concentrate on the contact list in my phone, deciding who to call next.

I call Wilson but it goes straight to voicemail and I leave a message, "Listen, Wilson, I've been evicted from my fucking apartment. I need a place to crash. Call me back."

As I scroll through my contact list I realize I'm running out of people to call already and wonder how I became such a recluse. I'd always been a people person, I tell myself, and pick at my upper lip until it finally falls away, leaving my upper row of teeth totally exposed. I see this in the mirror and recognize the problem. To rectify it, I pinch my bottom lip and yank and, like pink taffy, it stretches and eventually snaps and pulls away, exposing the bottom row of teeth for a good, healthy, and constant grin. I feel better just looking at myself in the mirror and feel that anyone else seeing me would also feel better. I look more approachable now, happier, upbeat, and personable. There's no doubt, I think, that people should like me even better now and be more willing to open their homes and lives to me and let me in, what with such a big grin as I have now.

However, everyone hangs up on me, from Syd and Lowry to Cleo, Stan, Gem, and even motherfucking Eric, though

I'm not sure why I even have that asshole's number. At this point I'd be willing to crash on Old Man Bill's floor but he doesn't have a phone of any sort, of course.

Then I remember to call Abigail but forget she's dead before pressing "send" on my phone. As the phone rings her old number a new woman picks up and I realize what I've done and start to cry, sickened by her absence and the ghost of a connection left in my phone's memory banks.

"Who is this?" the voice on the other end of the line asks. "Are you OK?"

"I… uh…" I say, sniffling and trying to choke back tears, unsuccessfully.

"Who is this? What's wrong? Why are you crying?" the voice asks, obviously concerned, and it touches me that someone knows anyone that could be concerned at the slightest sound of duress. If I was someone else… this concern, this sympathy might actually be directed at me. But I'm on the line with a dead girl and it's just not a possibility.

"I just… I just wanna go home, Abigail," I say, choking. "I'm so sick and lonely here by myself. I just wish I could fall off a cliff and be where you are—be with you. I'm falling apart here, Abigail. I'm losing everything I had left," I continue, recognizing my melodrama through my tears and embarrassing myself in front of the bartender standing a few feet away washing glasses but obviously listening.

"Luke? Is that you?"

Confused, and kind of shocked, I snort back a sob and say, "Huh? What?" while wiping my eyes and taking a gulp of my Jim Beam.

"Is that you, Luke? What's wrong?" the voice asks.

"Luke? No! No, it's not fucking *Luke*! Who the fuck is *Luke*? Who is this fucking *Luke*? Tell me!" I scream into the phone, holding it right in front of my lipless mouth before slamming the cheap cell down on the bar.

Instead of reflecting on why no one I know will help me out or even act like they know who I am, I sit in Harry's and drink Jim Beam after Jim Beam, which are generously comped to me for some reason, and smoke a whole pack of Winstons while watching sores open up all over my body. They redden, leak pus, blacken, and recede, revealing wet meat and tendons on my forearms and neck. The tickle in my crotch won't go away and when I reach down there I come away with my cock and balls, all dry and shriveled up, and I just let them drop to the ground, along with all the other skin layering the floor beneath me now. From time to time I laugh for no particular reason and look around myself to find that the bar is full of people that look like me and when they see me laugh they look me in the eye and also laugh lipless laughs and if they're close enough they might pat me on the back and keep laughing but they never tell me what they're laughing about and I'm not sure what I'm laughing about, either, and instead of it all making me feel better I feel the darkness wash over me in a wave of nausea.

And I just want to go home.

I've called everyone I know but one person, Cameron, who I haven't spoken to for weeks because she decided I was no good for her and that I was a bad influence on the kid. I of course told her that I was great for her and that there was nothing wrong with giving her kid a little bit of whiskey from time to time and taking him with me to the strip club for educational purposes or teaching him that everyone you meet is a monster, including your mother, and even your father if you ever find him. Besides, he was basically a teenager and a full-grown person, I said, and she said he was only seven or something and not remotely a teenager but I couldn't really be bothered to listen to her crazy rants so who knows.

Just as I'm about to call Cameron, the bartender says she's closing up and all the fucking zombies in the bar grunt and grumble and peel their rotting selves from their stools and chairs and shuffle out of the bar with drooped heads and shoulders.

"I've got just one call I need to make," I say, my eternal grin aimed directly at the fat bartender's face, which seems to be melting off in a technicolor drain.

"Oh, honey, take all the time you need," she says and it makes me feel good to be treated with such affection.

Clicking on Cameron's number I hear a phone ring, in echo. I realize it's because there's another phone ringing in the bar while I listen to the phone ringing in my ear, and then I see the bartender pick up her phone, glance at the screen, then back up at me, smiling that broken smile.

"Luke, why are you calling me?" she asks.

"Huh?" I ask, my ear to the phone, the ring in my ear and the ring in the room colliding against each other inside my head.

"Why are you calling me, silly?" she asks.

"Quiet," I say. "I'm trying to call a friend of mine."

She laughs and answers her phone and says hello and I say hello and she asks what I want and I say that I miss her and that I'm sorry that I disappointed her and she says that it's all in the past. With time, I tell her, I can be a good man and even a better father. The kid means something to me, I say, and family means something to me. She asks me to tell her what family means and I say blood. I say lots of blood. And she agrees. I tell her I need a place to stay. She says she has a place for me, that she always has a place for me, and I tell her I'm a monster, that I barely have the skin left to cover my ugliness. She says no problem, then hangs up, reaches under the bar, and pulls out a first aid kit and walks over to me and smoothes Neosporin all over my exposed meat before carefully wrapping my arms, hands, neck, and face in gauze. She says she'll take care of me just fine and kisses my teeth because I have no lips for her to kiss. When I start to cry she tells me it's going to be OK. It's all going to be OK. She promises. I feel my wounds dampen and darken my wrappings. She smiles again and her eyes twinkle and she pours one last whiskey down my throat before putting my cock and balls in a grease-soaked paper bag and taking me back to her place where she wraps all her loose and flabby flesh around my skinless body, covering me and comforting me until I finally understand what going home is all about.

Logan Ryan Smith is from California and currently lives in Chicago. He's had fiction published in *Hobart Journal*, *Meat for Tea: The Valley Review*, and *Great Lakes Review*, which nominated his story "Bret Easton Ellis" for a Pushcart Prize. Though he now focuses exclusively on fiction, his poetry books include *The Singers & The Notes* (Dusie Press, 2007), *Stupid Birds* (Transmission Press, 2007), and, most recently, *Bug House* (Mission Cleaners Books, 2013), a narrative series of poems about isolation that features fantasy elements similar to *Enjoy Me*. He plans to follow up *Enjoy Me* with a novel that revolves around the same main character.

CPSIA information can be obtained
at www.ICGtesting.com
Printed in the USA
BVHW032300170520
579835BV00001BA/37

9 781505 553338